A Candlelight Ecstasy Romance ™

"AFRAID?" HE TEASED SOFTLY.

The bitter answer her mind was framing was never expressed. His mouth descended on hers, locking her lips to his with a commanding force, flooding her body with feelings that had nothing to do with anger. By the time she thought of fighting him, his arms had encircled her body, holding her against his full length.

Men I don't like shouldn't kiss like this, she thought frantically, trying to remember how much he irritated her.

One firm hand caressed her lower back, sending off heat waves that made her squirm against him. She shuddered, hating herself for the weakness that kept her from fighting him. . . .

LOVE TRAP

Barbara Andrews

A CANDLELIGHT ECSTASY ROMANCE ™

Published by
Dell Publishing Co., Inc.
1 Dag Hammarskjold Plaza
New York, New York 10017

Dell ® TM 681510, Dell Publishing Co., Inc.
Candlelight Ecstasy Romance™ is a trademark of
Dell Publishing Co., Inc., New York, New York.

ISBN: 0-440-14601-1

Printed in the United States of America

First printing—October 1982

To Our Readers:

We have been delighted with your enthusiastic response to Candlelight Ecstasy Romances™ and we thank you for the interest you have shown in this exciting series.

In the upcoming months we will continue to present the distinctive, sensuous love stories you have come to expect only from Ecstasy. We look forward to bringing you many more books from your favorite authors, and also the very finest work from new authors of contemporary romantic fiction.

As always, we are striving to present the unique, absorbing love stories that you enjoy most—books that are more than ordinary romance.

Your suggestions and comments are always welcome. Please write to us at the address below.

Sincerely,

The Editors
Candlelight Romances
1 Dag Hammarskjold Plaza
New York, New York 10017

CHAPTER ONE

"Partner, I think this might be the right place," Dawn said, tipping the straw cowboy hat on the head of the very young man beside her on the car seat. "You stay here while I check the mailbox."

Closing the door of her little silver Honda so Gary wouldn't follow her, she sighed and crossed her fingers. This was the third mailbox she'd stopped to look at since the sun had disappeared below the horizon, and as grateful as she was not to have to drive directly into the blinding glare anymore, she was getting more and more worried as the light faded with each passing mile. She and her three-year-old traveling companion had crossed the Mississippi River several hours earlier, and driving between endless fields of Iowa corn, the stalks higher than a man's head, was becoming unnerving. One road looked much the same as all the others, and trying to follow the map Sheila had scrawled on a wrinkled scrap of brown bag was frustrating at best.

Sheila Gilbert! How could any woman abandon her child? Just thinking about the callousness of her neighbor could bring tears to Dawn's eyes, but she had more immediate concerns. Even if she managed to find Gary's father tonight, she still had a long drive in order to reach a town large enough to have a motel where she could stay the night; she might have to drive another hour through the maze of cornfields.

7

The sharply stenciled name on the oversized metal mailbox was done in bold block letters, and by daylight it would have been easy to see:

EVAN CRANE
Route 4

At least this solved Dawn's major problem. She could leave Gary with his father and pray that this parent would care more for him than his mother did.

"This is where your daddy lives, Gary," she said as gaily as possible. "Just think, you're going to live on a real farm."

"Will you live there too?" Gary asked for the hundredth time as she started the car again.

"Honey, you know I have to go to California. Your mommy just asked me to bring you to your daddy, but you're going to have a wonderful time here. Maybe your daddy has a dog you can play with. He's a farmer, and farmers sometimes have pigs and cows and chickens too."

Dawn felt uncomfortable suggesting things to Gary that might not be true, but she wanted desperately to help him adjust to a father he didn't seem to remember. During her two years of working for the Welfare Department, she'd listened to accounts of all kinds of human misery, but it still made her heartsick when a child was unwanted. Hopefully Gary's father would be different from his mother.

The gravel road just beyond the mailbox threaded its way between two cornfields, their giant green stalks seeming to sway toward the slow-moving car. Dawn hoped Gary's fantasies didn't include plants that reached out to grab people, and decided she was being more childish than he was. She was bringing a little boy safely to his father; then her responsibility would end. There was no reason on earth for the growing sense of uneasiness she'd felt since finding the mailbox.

The entry road was longer than she'd expected, and the house that sat beyond the last bend was a total surprise. Dawn had imagined a big box of a house with narrow wooden siding, or maybe even a delightfully spooky Victorian relic with gingerbread trim and long slender windows with shades that winked like eyelids when they were lowered. Instead, this farmhouse might qualify for a spread in *Better Homes and Gardens,* if what she could see of the long, low, ranch-style structure lived up to its promise in the daylight. Giant spruce trees scattered around the house relieved the monotony of the surrounding cornfields, their low branches serving as the perfect place for a young boy to play. Certainly Gary would have a better life here than in a crowded little apartment.

"Well, here we are, Gary." She hoped her cheerfulness didn't sound as forced to Gary as it did to her own ears.

In spite of the appealing setting her doubts were growing and, unfortunately, she wasn't reassured by the fact that the windows of the house were totally dark.

"Is my daddy here?" Gary removed the oversized hat from his pale blond head and peered apprehensively through the open car windows.

"It doesn't look like he's home yet, honey, but farmers work late during the summer. We'll just wait awhile, and I'm sure he'll come home."

Dawn had tried to call Evan Crane countless times on the busy, confusing day before they'd left Pittsburgh, but he had never answered the phone. She wished there'd been time to write a letter saying that Gary was coming, but the last thing she'd expected when she made her plans to go to Los Angeles had been a three-year-old passenger. Once on the road, it had seemed futile to continue trying to call. Her secret fear was that Gary's father would tell her not to bring him, and then what on earth would she do with the boy she'd only agreed to keep for a weekend? He would have to become a ward of the state, and no one knew better than a social worker how harrowing that could be for a young child. It was far better to gamble that he had a caring father in Iowa. Otherwise, if his mother never claimed him, Gary could grow up being shuffled from one foster home to another, and Dawn cared too much about him to let that happen.

Arriving at a dark house was a nuisance, but fortunately they'd stopped at a fast-food place just after entering Iowa, so neither of them was hungry. Yet, if Gary was as tired as she was, he needed to be in bed.

"Let's walk around a little, Gary," Dawn suggested.

He had to be coaxed to leave the security of the car, but once freed from the seat belt, he ran up and down the gravel drive, enjoying the crunchy sound his feet made, but always coming back to Dawn when the distance between them became threatening. She picked him up and hugged him several times, knowing it would be hard to say good-bye to him.

When Gary tired of the gravel drive, they walked over the broad expanse of grass in front of the house, but the mosquitoes discovered their presence and attacked in force. Dawn picked Gary up after she felt the first stinging bites on her bare ankles, but she soon realized that they couldn't stay outside and be bitten again and again. Since she'd left the car windows open, there'd probably be a swarm of the little monsters inside the car too. The only alternative was to find shelter in the house or in one of the outbuildings.

As she expected, no one answered when she knocked repeatedly on the front door; apparently farmers didn't have a need for doorbells, but anyone inside could have heard her pounding. There was no shelter in the front of the house, so she hurried around to the back, still carrying Gary, who seemed to gain weight with each step she took.

A huge screened-in patio dominated the rear of the house, and, much to her relief, the door wasn't locked. In the city opening the door might be considered trespassing, but here it was urgent to take cover. She and Gary must have disturbed a whole colony of bugs, and they couldn't stay outside to be a walking feast for a million bloodthirsty demons.

The moon was high in a cloudless sky, and several inviting lounge chairs were scattered around inside the screened area. Dawn thought she'd feel and look less like a sneak-thief if she turned on a light, so she deposited Gary on the nearest chair and moved cautiously to the wall of the house, hoping to find a switch. Sliding doors led to the interior of the house, but there didn't seem to be an outside switch. She touched the handle on one door and was surprised to feel it slide an inch or so. Iowa farmers were nothing if not trusting! She couldn't imagine leaving such an attractive house unlocked in the city.

"I have to go potty."

Gary's voice, sounding sleepy and quarrelsome, repeated his request a second and a third time before Dawn could decide what to do. He could go outside, she supposed, but that meant more nasty bites for both of them. Her legs itched in a dozen places, and one bite on her elbow was a torment. She'd have to gamble that they could use the bathroom and get out of the house again before the owner came home. Heaven help them if he were asleep inside! She desperately hoped it was too early for even early-to-rise farmers to be in bed.

The sliding doors were actually double doors, and she had to open both the glass and the screen to gain entry. The floor plan was a complete mystery, so she had no choice but to grope for a light switch.

When she found the right switch, recessed flood lamps in the ceiling revealed a large room done in restful neutral shades of beige, brown, and rust. Textured wallpaper har-

11

monized with walnut paneling, while massive crocks were planted with an assortment of green giants. A fireplace made of huge stones, each chipped to reveal the rough natural beauty of the minerals, dominated the room. It was a place for friendly companionship and close relationships, and she felt that the man who lived in it must be a warm, caring person.

It seemed less like intruding to go into the kitchen area and find the small half-bath there than to search the bedroom wing of the house. Returning to the family room, she knew they should wait outside on the patio, but the big, quilted couch was just too inviting. Since his father lived here, wasn't it Gary's home too? Surely Evan Crane wouldn't object if they waited in the family room for him.

The long day of traveling caught up with Gary quickly, and in only minutes he was sound asleep at one end of the couch, his cowboy hat abandoned on the floor.

Dawn smothered a yawn, but her eyes were drooping with fatigue. It wasn't long before she dozed off unintentionally; not even the prospect of embarrassment if she were found sleeping in a stranger's house was enough to fight back her weariness after so many hours of driving.

She awoke slowly with a nagging feeling that something was wrong. Her eyes found Gary first, but he was peacefully sleeping, curled into a half-ball at the end of the couch. Rubbing the sleep from her eyes, she sat upright.

"Unless you're Goldilocks and I'm Papa Bear, we have a big problem," a voice said sarcastically from across the room.

"Oh," Dawn said, struggling to pull down the once-crisp beige skirt that had ridden up on her shapely thighs while she slept.

"Just tell me one thing," he said, moving closer. "What the hell are you doing in my house?"

Dawn looked at him speechlessly; surely the man could see that she had his son with her. She had a moment of sheer panic, thinking that she had come into the wrong house. Gary's father was a farmer; this man would look at home in a law office or a corporation conference room. Even in casual clothes he looked like a polished executive. Everything about him was trim, with broad shoulders tapering to a slim waist and narrow hips. He was tall, but not excessively so, and only his sun-bleached hair and deeply tanned face suggested that he might be a person who worked outdoors.

He interpreted her surprise as a guilty silence and said, "You can explain to the sheriff, if you'd rather."

"The mosquitoes were terrible, so I didn't think you'd mind if we waited inside. Your door wasn't locked."

"There's never been any reason to lock doors out here. Usually all my guests are invited."

"I tried to call before we started out, but you never answered the phone," Dawn explained, hating herself for sounding so muddled. "I didn't have much notice, you see, and once we were on the road, it seemed futile to keep trying."

"Please, miss, I'm tired, and whatever you're trying to say isn't coming through. Just tell me why you're here, then get out."

"Get out! I certainly will, but you could thank me for bringing your son all the way from Pittsburgh."

"I don't have a son."

"Oh, no! Aren't you Evan Crane?"

"Yes."

"But I've brought Gary to you. My God, Sheila didn't tell me you'd never seen him. Oh, how could she do this!"

"Sheila?"

"Sheila Gilbert. She was my neighbor in the apartment down the hall. I only agreed to take care of Gary for the weekend, so when she didn't come home, I was frantic. I had the landlord check her apartment, and that's when I found these."

13

She pulled the note and Sheila's crude map from her purse and handed them to the stern-faced man.

"Dear Dawn," he read aloud, "I can't take care of Gary anymore. I know you're going to California to look for a new job and all, so please, please, please take him to his father in Iowa. I looked at a map and it's right on your way, and he won't be any trouble at all in the car."

Her only signature was a large, sprawling initial.

"I'm Dawn Lounsbury," Dawn said weakly when Evan's silent gaze seemed to be analyzing every detail of her person. "It just seemed like the only thing to do, bringing him here. I'm a social worker; I knew how he'd be shuffled around if I turned him over to the authorities."

Evan walked closer to the end of the couch, where Gary was still sleeping, but his searching appraisal wasn't at all reassuring.

"If I'd even suspected that your wife—" she began.

"My wife is dead," he said, interrupting curtly without looking away from the sleeping child. "Did Sheila pay you to bring this kid here?"

"Of course not!"

"No, I suppose a sad story would be enough, if you are a social worker."

"I am, but that doesn't make me stupid. I lived in the same building with Gary for two years. I—"

She was going to say that she cared very much what happened to him, but this man didn't invite emotional confidences.

"What's the bottom line?" he demanded. "Is Sheila using you to get support money?"

"At least you do know her."

"She was my sister-in-law," he said irritably. "Well, is it money she wants?"

"I don't know anything about that," Dawn said, her own anger growing. "What I've told you is all that I know."

"You expect me to believe that you took someone else's child out of his home state to leave him with a stranger?"

"Only because his mother left me no choice."

"Or was it because you're so used to meddling in other people's lives that it's become a habit?"

"I don't meddle! This is between you and Sheila."

"Where is she?"

"If I knew that, I wouldn't have brought Gary here," she said, her own exasperation beginning to match his.

He reached down to pick up Gary's cowboy hat, turning it over as if it were an alien artifact. His hands, she noticed, were unusually large, but his fingers were slender. His touch on the frail little hat was light, but it still managed to suggest latent power. A totally inappropriate thought popped into her head: *How would it feel to have those hands touch her?* She shuddered, but not from repugnance.

"Well, he's here, isn't he, whether he's mine or not. Let's put him to bed, and we'll talk this out."

"There's nothing more to say. I've told you all I know."

"I'll decide that," he said, bending to lift the sleeping child.

Gary stirred and opened his eyes for a moment, but he was too sleepy to react to the strange face above him. Dawn followed the pair down a carpeted hallway into a large, square room.

"My housekeeper keeps the sheets in the bottom bureau drawer," he said, his tone ordering her to find them.

He held Gary on his shoulder with no apparent strain while Dawn made up the big double bed. She felt unaccountably awkward as she tried to fit the stylish maroon and gray striped sheets onto the mattress. The man made small noises of impatience, but he didn't say anything. When the bed was made, he lowered the sleeping child and left him there, leaving Dawn to pull off his canvas shoes and tuck him in.

15

At least he didn't order us out of the house, Dawn thought as she trailed Evan Crane back to the spacious family room. If only she could be sure he'd accept responsibility for Gary, she'd leave immediately. The whole situation was terribly uncomfortable, and she was beginning to doubt her own common sense in bringing Gary.

He turned abruptly to face Dawn when she came into the room behind him, making her even more aware of what an attractive man he was. His scent suggested open fields, fresh air, and newly cut grass, and the eyes that held hers without wavering were a color of their own, neither green nor brown, but an intriguing and varying shade of hazel. He was the kind of man who made a woman forget her own plans and ambitions, Dawn realized, belatedly erecting barriers to keep him at a distance. Her life was complicated enough at this point without letting herself be attracted to a man who was proving to be an adversary. The sooner she left, the better.

"Sit down," he ordered.

She did, but only to save time.

"You've brought a child here that Sheila Gilbert gave you," he began.

"Sheila abandoned him," she quickly corrected him.

He ignored her comment and went on.

"Are you sure Sheila was his mother?"

"She said she was, but . . ."

Dawn hesitated. Should she tell this hostile man what kind of a mother Sheila was? The consensus of most of the people in the building was that Gary was a hardy child to have survived Sheila's indifferent care. His meals were irregular and rarely nourishing, except when he went to a day-care center, his clothes and person were usually dirty and unkempt, and a friendly older woman in the building had finally taken over the job of toilet-training when his filthy diapers became too obvious to the other tenants.

16

"There's something you don't want to tell me," he said, his eyes alert to Dawn's hesitation.

"Well, Sheila wasn't a very good mother," she said reluctantly.

His laugh wasn't pleasant. "You didn't need to tell me that. Sheila never cared about anyone but herself. Did she say where Gary was born?"

Well, at least he's using Gary's name instead of calling him "kid," Dawn thought, but she said, "They came to Pittsburgh from Chicago, but she was always a little vague about the past."

"I'll bet she was!"

"Mr. Crane, I have to know. Can Gary be your child?"

"Not if Sheila Gilbert is his mother," he answered angrily.

"But if she isn't?" Dawn persisted.

He turned and walked to the sliding doors, obviously trying to decide how to answer that question.

"How old is Gary?" he asked.

"He was three in June."

"Then it's possible," he said, drawing in breath sharply and releasing it slowly, keeping his back turned and thrusting his hands into his pockets.

"Then Gary is your son?"

"Damn it, how would I know?" He turned to face her. "My wife, Peg, and I separated before Christmas, and she got a quickie divorce in Mexico. It would have been like her not to tell me she was pregnant. She knew how much I wanted a child."

The bitterness in his voice said more than his words, and Dawn didn't know what else to say.

"I can't understand why Sheila would keep him this long if he is mine." He was talking more to himself than Dawn. "More likely he's Sheila's, and she's tired of playing mother. It would be like her to try to unload her responsibilities on me."

17

He paced back and forth in front of Dawn, making her all too aware of the energy and alertness in his body. When he came out of himself and addressed her directly, she had to force herself to keep her mind on Gary.

"How did Sheila live?" he asked.

"She had a job in a clothing store."

"No, I mean what was her standard of living? Fancy clothes, car, that sort of thing?"

"I really didn't know her well. Mostly she just came by to ask favors."

Dawn ran her fingers through her short chestnut-brown curls, a sure giveaway to anyone who knew her that she was nervous.

"But you knew her well enough, I take it, for her to dump a kid on you for the weekend. Did she pay you for baby-sitting?"

"No, she offered once, but I refused. I really enjoyed having Gary, and I liked to be able to keep a check on how he was doing."

"Okay, so Gary was your personal charity, but did Sheila need it?"

Dawn considered his question and responded thoughtfully.

"When I first moved there, I would have said no. She had new car, a beautiful wardrobe, lots of really sharp clothes. And jewelry—pieces that looked valuable. I hadn't thought much about it, but she wasn't buying new clothes lately or wearing her better jewelry. She seemed to be having a harder time, but, as far as anyone knew, she still had her job."

"Probably what happened is that she ran out of insurance money. Peg had a good policy that I bought for her. It would have paid double for her car accident. She didn't die immediately, so she could have made her sister promise to keep the child. When the money ran out, Sheila

18

probably forgot about promises and decided to unload the boy on me."

"Then you do think Gary is your son?" Dawn couldn't conceal the relief in her voice.

"How the devil would I know?" he stormed, directing his frustration at her. "Maybe Sheila's trying to get rid of her own illegitimate son. You're a social worker. Why didn't you investigate and get some answers before you started playing with people's lives?"

The unfairness of his accusation stunned her.

"I thought I was bringing Gary to a father who would be delighted to have him."

"Sure, it's the middle of summer, I have nine hundred acres of corn and soybeans to worry about with no rain for a month, and I'm supposed to take care of a kid who may or may not be mine."

"There must be someone who can help you."

"My mother moved to Arizona after my father died, my sister lives in Oregon, and my housekeeper only comes twice a week."

"You'll figure out something," she snapped angrily, standing to face him.

As upset as she was, one compartment of her mind noted that he was the perfect height for her, topping her five and a half feet by a comfortable six inches or so.

"I already have," he said grimly.

"Good, then I'll bring in Gary's things and leave while there's still a possibility of finding a motel to stay in tonight."

"No, you won't."

"Won't find a place? I thought I could get to Des Moines in less than an hour."

"You won't leave."

"I certainly will. I have a friend expecting me in Los Angeles. I'm behind schedule already."

"He'll have to wait. You're staying right here until this thing is settled one way or another."

"My friend is a she, and I can't possibly stay."

She snatched her purse from the floor by the end of the couch and moved toward the sliding doors, but she wasn't nearly fast enough. He caught her wrist and stepped to block her way.

"You can't keep me here against my will," she cried out.

"Can't I? There's still the trespassing charge, and I played high school football with the sheriff."

"That is a mean, underhanded threat. I dare you to call your friend the sheriff. A night in jail would be better than being a prisoner here."

"I don't have to call anyone," he said, smiling unpleasantly. "You won't get far without these."

The car keys he pulled out of the pocket of his snug-fitting tan slacks were unmistakably hers. Knowing that he'd searched her purse made her temper flare.

"You had no right to go into my purse."

"Why not? You walked into my house uninvited. I'd say we're even."

"I was trying to help Gary."

"Look, Dawn, you brought a child here, and you're going to be responsible for him until I learn the truth. You can stay here and take care of him, or you can take him with you."

"You'd let your own son go?"

"I don't know that he is my son."

"You can hire a baby-sitter until you're sure."

"All right, if that's the way you want it, you're hired. I should have known a friend of Sheila's would think of money first."

"I don't want your money or your job. That's not the point at all. I have to go to California."

"It will still be there in a few days or so, however long

20

it takes to trace Gary's birth records. Unless there's an earthquake, that is. Why do you want to go to California?"

"For a better job, of course," she said furiously. "My college roommate is working for social services in L.A. The girl who was sharing her apartment got married, so she asked me to come live with her. I have a Spanish language minor, so she was sure I could find a job there in my field."

"So you're running off to California without a job offer. What was wrong with the job you had?"

"A computer could have replaced me. All I did was take down facts from welfare applicants and write reports. It was a totally impersonal job, nothing like what I expected when I went into social work."

"Not enough personal involvement?" he challenged her.

"I guess you could put it that way."

"Well, you're involved now, up to your pretty neck. Just think of Gary as one of your clients."

"I cannot stay here." She tried to sound calm and professional, but her emotions betrayed her.

"You can and will. Call your friend."

"She can't afford to pay double rent very long. She's expecting me by Sunday."

"Then she's going to be disappointed. You're staying right here until this thing is settled." His voice was low and controlled, but he jammed her keys into his pants pocket with a violence that betrayed his agitation.

Their eyes met, his steely and unwavering, hers dark and on the verge of filling with tears of frustration. Before she could decide what to do next, he took the initiative from her.

"Come to your car with me and show me what you need for tonight. I'll bring in the rest in the morning."

He led her through the broad main hallway and out the

front door, walking so rapidly that she didn't have time to think about the vicious mosquitoes that had driven her into his house. She pointed out the two grocery bags that held all of Gary's possessions, struck by the poignancy of the child's situation. All he had in the world was in those bags, and she had all but promised him a loving father.

With a minimum of words she indicated that all she needed was her small overnight case. He dumped one of the bags into her arms and turned toward the house, carrying the rest. He relocked the car and put the keys back into his pocket.

"You can have my mother's room," he said ungraciously. "She's too busy trying to get her life masters in bridge to put in an appearance this summer."

"Doesn't your mother miss your congenial company?" Dawn asked, baiting him.

He laughed, but it was a cold, superficial sound. "She had thirty-seven years on the farm. I guess she deserves to play a little now."

"I can understand that thirty-seven years of your company would be enough for any woman." Dawn knew this sounded trite, but she had to strike back at him somehow. Why, he was virtually taking her prisoner, and all she had tried to do was reunite a father and son.

"My wife didn't last thirty-seven months," he said harshly. "It takes a special kind of woman to live a rural life."

His tone told her very plainly that she was among those who couldn't hack it. He pushed open a door across from the room where Gary was sleeping, letting her follow him into it. Dumping his burden on the plush, cream-colored carpet, he gestured toward a door on the right.

"The bathroom connects with my room too. If you don't like to be surprised, remember to lock the door." He started to shut the door, but did not complete the action.

The grimace he made let Dawn know that he was just

22

as unhappy with the situation as she was. Before she had a chance to look around the room, the door flew open.

"Sheets are in the bottom bureau drawer in here too. I have to pick up a work crew in town at seven, so I'll be gone before you're awake. Help yourself in the kitchen. Mrs. Winsch comes around eight."

"Then why can't Mrs. Winsch take care of Gary?" Dawn asked.

"I told you, she only comes twice a week," he said angrily, slamming the door loudly.

A choice word escaped her mouth, but it didn't make her feel any better. She did feel responsible for Gary, and, even worse, leaving him at any time was going to be sad. If she was forced to be with him longer, it would make it all the harder to part with him. If Evan Crane wasn't such an insensitive egotist, he'd see that the longer she stayed, the worse the trauma of their parting would be for Gary.

What about leaving his father? The question came into her mind unbidden and wouldn't be pushed aside. She was honest enough with herself to admit that all the chemistry was right between them, but she couldn't allow herself any complications just when her career seemed to be taking an upswing. The small inheritance that she'd received from her grandmother's estate last year was just enough to make a fresh start in a more challenging and promising job. It wouldn't last long, but while it did, it spelled opportunity.

Once before she'd had to choose between her own plans and ambitions and a man; she didn't want that kind of pain again. When Jim Turner had asked her to marry him, the catch had been more than she could handle. Saying yes would have meant giving up her own career and going with him to a remote area of Wyoming where he had a job as a mining engineer. Naturally he had been eager for a wife to look after him there, but the prospect of endless days with nothing constructive to do proved to be a testing ground for Dawn's love. Her feelings failed the test; she hadn't loved Jim enough to give up her own dreams, to spend months or even years trying to keep busy in a mobile home.

The whole situation was Sheila's fault. They had never been friends, and Dawn had been cordial to her only because it gave her more opportunity to see that Gary was all right. It was common knowledge that Sheila had left him alone at times when he was still an infant, and the care she gave him in general was only marginally acceptable. As a trained professional, Dawn felt obligated to watch out for his welfare, or at least that was what she firmly believed. Evan Crane had called her a meddler, but where was the dividing line between helping and interfering?

Belatedly she noticed how pleasant the bedroom was, with its color scheme of cream and cocoa-brown accented by brightly woven Apache rugs hung on the walls. It wasn't a room that could be considered feminine in taste, but the furnishings did show that the occupant had a lively interest in many things. A long set of shelves nearly covered one wall and held a variety of figurines and artifacts, apparently from cultures all over the world.

Dawn went over to admire an Eskimo scene carved in a solid chunk of glass. Whatever her preconceived notions of a farmer's wife had been, Evan Crane's mother certainly didn't fit them. She must be a traveler and an art enthusiast to have gathered so many lovely things. Dawn couldn't understand why she didn't keep her treasures near her in her retirement home, unless this was only part of her collection. She picked up a small bronze figurine that resembled a Greek athlete, then was embarrassed by her idle handling of it. The little man was stark naked, and she had subconsciously compared his body to that of her jailer-host.

The way her thoughts were going, the safest thing to do was go to bed. After hurriedly digging out her nightgown and toothbrush, she went to use the bathroom. Not until she tried the door and found it locked did she remember that the bath was connected with the master bedroom. After waiting a few minutes, she heard the shower, then it seemed like ages before total silence indicated that the room was empty.

The bathroom was warm and steamy, with a pleasant smell of masculine cologne lingering in the air. Even though Evan had left the room as neat as she could wish, reminders of his recent presence lingered.

Dawn hurried through her evening routine, not forgetting to lock the door that led to his room. She had many reasons for being ill at ease, but she didn't want to stay awake analyzing them any longer than necessary.

She was in bed with the lights out when she remembered Gary. Surely a good mother checked on her child before going to sleep herself. Dawn didn't want to act the mother's role in the little boy's life, that was for sure, but she did find she couldn't relax until she looked in on him.

Stepping silently into the dark hallway on bare feet, she moved across to Gary's room, easing the door open so she wouldn't wake him. The gasp in her throat nearly escaped when the dark figure leaning over Gary straightened.

"Oh, you frightened me," she whispered breathlessly. "I came to check on Gary."

"He's fine," Evan said curtly, brushing past her in the doorway so the sleeve of his slightly damp terry robe touched her bare arm.

So I caught you taking another look at your son, she thought with some malice. Maybe Mr. Crane wasn't so hard-hearted after all. Still, a little voice warned her not to count on it.

CHAPTER TWO

Dawn awoke from dreams so vivid, it didn't seem as if she'd been sleeping, but they were instantly forgotten when she managed to identify the sound that had roused her as water running. Remembering where she was, she knew that Evan was just behind the bathroom door, and further sleep was impossible.

Her host, of course, was getting ready for his day. She squinted at her wristwatch on the bedside table, and wasn't too pleased to see that it was only five thirty. After yesterday's trying drive and her clash with Evan, she'd hoped to sleep at least until Gary woke her. No wonder the rural life wasn't for just any woman, as Evan had pointed out. She hated to agree with him on anything, but it certainly wasn't for her.

Surprisingly she did feel well rested, and with the return of her high energy level, she felt doubly rebellious. There was a whole world out there waiting for her, and there wasn't any way Evan Crane could keep her here against her will, even if he'd played football with the whole sheriff's department.

Quickly dressing in jeans and a shirt from her suitcase, she dashed cold water on her face and brushed her teeth. Maybe if she confronted Crane drinking his coffee, he'd be more congenial than he was after a day of whatever it was farmers do. He'd caught her at a low ebb last night, that's all. It hadn't been easy to drive steadily cross-country when she wasn't used to it, and entertaining a three-year-old in a car was a job in itself. Because his mother had paid so little attention to Gary, he was pretty unruly at times.

The coffee created an aromatic trail to the kitchen, enhanced by bacon fumes and the sound of dishes being laid.

"Good morning," she said with forced cheerfulness.

"I didn't expect you up this early," he said rather grudgingly, "but there's enough for two."

"You aren't the quietest neighbor I've ever had," she said, feeling she owed him something for his lack of enthusiasm.

"Sorry, I've gotten used to living alone."

"Actually that's what I need to talk about."

"Have some breakfast first. I'm a bear in the morning until I've had something to eat."

So much for catching him in a good mood, Dawn thought ruefully.

He managed to set a second place, finish the bacon, and fry some eggs before she even got her thoughts organized. No wonder his wife left him, she mused. No one could stand that much efficiency so early in the morning.

The coffee was clear and mellow, just the way she liked it, and the crisp bacon didn't have a smidgen of fat in it. Even her egg was a perfect sunny-side up. She decided if he brought out freshly made blueberry muffins, she'd scream; toasting bread was a big chore for her in the morning.

There weren't any muffins, but his toast was made with thick dark slices of whole-wheat bread. She didn't pass up the fresh honey, either, and when she smeared it on a second piece, he actually smiled. There were tiny laugh lines by his eyes that she hadn't noticed before, and his nose was an engineering marvel, straight and firm without protruding unduly. Trying to decide why it was such a fine example of a nose made her lose her train of thought

27

again, and a sticky drop of honey slid down her chin. To her surprise, he reached across the table and wiped it away with his napkin.

"My mother never throws anything away," he was saying. "Look around in the basement. You're sure to find some of my old toys down there. I've seen an old rocking horse lately, I know. Bring up whatever you need to keep Gary entertained."

"Mr. Crane," she said, smiling with what she hoped was appeal, "is there any real reason—"

"Call me Evan," he interrupted.

"Evan, is there any reason why you couldn't hire a real baby-sitter, maybe a high school girl who needs a summer job? I'm a professional person, not a nanny."

"You're wasting your breath. You're staying here."

"You just cannot keep me here against my will to take care of your son."

"I wouldn't keep you here to take care of my son, but neither of us knows whether he is mine. What happens if his birth records show he's Sheila's? Then he becomes your problem. Until we know, you stay right here."

"He'd still be your nephew!"

"I severed all connection with my ex-wife and her dippy sister. If Sheila's counting on that tie, she's out of luck."

"You're talking about a small, defenseless boy."

"You are. I'm talking about investigations and proof and responsibility."

He got up from the table, scowling, and his expression did more to intimidate her than his words.

"You are absolutely heartless!" Her voice became a little shrill when she yelled, so she made a tremendous effort to keep it low.

"One more thing, my little social worker. If I learn that you've conspired with Sheila Gilbert to saddle me with her kid, your sweet little behind will be on the line, and I'll be the one to blister it."

He didn't stay there to see the bright pink flush of fury rise to Dawn's cheeks, or to see her squirm on the seat of the kitchen chair. Even if he was talking figuratively, the thought of Evan Crane paddling her rear made her flex her buttocks uncomfortably. He was an insufferable, impossible man, and she'd see who would have the last word.

Gary slept late and awoke a bit bewildered by his new surroundings. He did hit it off immediately with the pleasant, round-faced woman who came to clean house. Unaccustomed as he was to special attention from his mother, he delighted in Mrs. Winsch's offer to make eggs-in-a-basket for his breakfast and watched carefully as she cut out a circle of bread with the rim of a drinking glass, frying the egg inside the remaining bread. The fried circle of bread became a cover for the "basket," and he ate every bite.

It was Mrs. Winsch, too, who took Gary to the basement to rummage for old toys, then let him help her clean them. Dawn felt totally superfluous, although she knew Gary would only have Mrs. Winsch twice a week.

"Did Mr. Crane talk to you about coming every day?" she asked casually over a lunch also prepared by Mrs. Winsch.

"Oh, dear, no. He knows I couldn't possibly do that," the older woman explained. "I've worked for the Bursens longer than Mr. Crane. It wouldn't be fair to them."

Satisfied that Evan had been truthful about his domestic arrangements, Dawn put Gary in his room for a nap and wandered outside to see what she could see. Except for the cornfields that seemed to be thriving in every direction, the place didn't match her idea of a farm at all. For one thing, there were no animals, which would disappoint Gary when he remembered her speculations, and the huge, steel-sided barn seemed to be used mainly to store and to maintain farm equipment. The early afternoon heat hung in a glaring shield over everything, and the grass underfoot was losing its color from the summer dry spell. When she tired of aimless wandering, she went back to the air-conditioned comfort of the house.

There was a large television set in the family room and several amply stocked bookshelves, but she couldn't generate any enthusiasm for passive recreation, even though she never had time to read as much as she liked. Thoughts of Evan Crane made her pace restlessly, trying to find a solution that would let her leave without jeopardizing Gary's future. Outside, she had confirmed for herself that her car was parked in the shade of the maintenance barn and was still locked, which only made her feel more overpowered by Evan's stubbornness. For a man who didn't lock his house, he was overly protective of her property; of course, he was guaranteeing that she wouldn't use the car for her escape.

If she couldn't take her car with her, she wasn't likely to leave, but she leafed through the phone book anyway to check on bus and taxi service in the area. She was thinking of calling a few, when the sliding door opened.

"Calling for help?" Evan asked in a definitely unfriendly tone.

"I've considered it."

"And decided?"

"That you have no right to keep my car keys."

"You're concerned with rights? How about responsibilities? Where's Mrs. Winsch?"

"In the basement, doing laundry."

"Did she show you how to use the machines in case you need to do extra loads for you and the kid?"

"No, I can figure it out myself, and please don't call Gary the kid."

"I stand corrected." He almost smiled.

"What are you doing here?" she asked.

"I live here."

"I mean at this time of day."

"If you've been outside, you know it's hot enough to boil a person's brains. I had my foreman, Dewey Clatt, truck our detasseling crew back to town. We start early in the morning, so they can quit when the heat builds up too much. I don't want kids passing out in my fields."

"What's a detasseling crew?"

"Mostly kids from about age fourteen through college."

"I mean, what's detasseling?"

"Pulling off tassels on female corn."

"Why?"

"Do you really want a lesson on growing hybrid corn?"

"No."

"Then I'll clean up and eat."

He walked away, leaving her to fume, but she felt curiously abandoned after he left. She idly leafed through a couple of farming magazines lying on the coffee table without seeing or caring to see anything in them. When Evan came back into the family room, he was wearing white shorts that showed his muscular legs to be marvelously well-proportioned and lightly tanned. She decided his clothing change had no effect whatsoever on her, and buried her face in the magazine she was holding.

"There's a good article in there on cutworm control," he said sarcastically.

"If there's nothing else to read, I'll read can labels," she said in a frosty tone.

"Well, it's nice that you have cosmopolitan interests."

"And also no concern of yours."

"Since we're going to be living together for a while, don't you think we could call a truce?"

His smile annoyed her more than his words.

"We are not 'living together' as you put it, and you have no right to keep me here."

"We're back to rights, are we?" His tone remained deceptively pleasant. "What right did you have taking over my couch last night with your skirt up around your neck?"

"It was not!"

"Just be happy I didn't take advantage of your display. The invitation was clear enough."

"I don't have to listen to this!"

She stood abruptly, throwing the rolled-up magazine at the table, but missing. Without stopping to pick it up, she headed for the hallway, hoping to escape to her room, but he was too quick, blocking her way with his body.

"Of course, that could be part of your plan too," he said wryly.

"I don't know what you're talking about. The only plan I have is to leave here."

"I'm not a poor man, as Sheila must have told you. More wealth comes out of Iowa soil every year than all the gold mines in the world."

"If you expect that to impress me, you're crazy!" She was shouting now, not caring if her voice did get shrill. "I'm trying to help Gary find a better life. If you can't believe that, we'll both leave. Some men make lousy fathers, and you certainly seem to be one of them. I'll keep Gary myself."

"How will you manage that?" he asked, sounding angry himself now. "You haven't a single legal claim to that child, and you know it."

"Love is more important than legal papers."

He smiled slightly, seemingly throwing off anger easily, a reaction that only annoyed her more.

"That's an interesting theory. Is that how you feel about marriage licenses too?" he challenged.

He was so close, his knee grazed her bare leg, the soft hair sending electric tingles through her. She backed away instinctively, but the wall blocked her retreat as his arms shot out to imprison her.

"Let me go," she whispered furiously, conscious that

they were right outside the room where Gary was napping.

"Your keys are in my right pocket," he said suggestively. "Take them if you want them."

His shorts were tailored with pockets like regular slacks, but Dawn knew she couldn't reach into one, not even to retrieve her keys. He would take such an intimate gesture as an invitation, and things were already speeding out of control.

"Afraid?" he teased softly.

The bitter answer her mind was framing was never expressed. His mouth descended on hers, locking her lips to his with a commanding force, flooding her body with feelings that had nothing to do with anger. By the time she thought of fighting him, his arms had circled her body, holding her against his full length.

Men I don't like shouldn't kiss like this, she thought frantically, trying to remember how much he irritated her.

One firm hand caressed her lower back, sending off heat waves that made her squirm against him, and his kisses explored the curvature of her chin, finding a sensually sensitive target just under her ear. She shuddered, hating herself for the weakness that kept her from fighting him.

It was as if a stranger were inhabiting her body, responding to the undisguised demands of a man she barely knew. Part of her cringed in embarrassment when an involuntary moan escaped from her throat, but she couldn't summon enough resolve to break free, not even when his hand cupped her buttocks and pressed her against him with an intimacy that made her light-headed. When his lips moved to hers again, she was dizzy with surprise at her reaction.

"Dawn, can I get up now?"

Gary's wide-awake howl acted like a sword slicing them apart instantly. Evan paused for only a second, taking in the damp flush he had caused on her face and the dazed

33

expression in her eyes, then he was gone. Apparently his appetite for food was forgotten; she heard the side door off the kitchen bang shut after him before she went into Gary's room. Sinking down on the edge of the bed, she helped him tie his shoes, but it took a long while for her shakiness to disappear.

Mrs. Winsch left promptly at five, having accomplished an impressive amount of work, including most of the preparations for dinner. Dawn didn't know if Evan would return to share the large pot roast with baby potatoes, onions, and carrots; she didn't even know if she dared to face him after so foolishly losing control of herself. As it was, his movements were out of her control too. He came back to the house before six o'clock, acting as if nothing had happened between them, calmly treating her as a casual houseguest.

His nonchalance was almost as maddening as his refusal to let her leave; Dawn didn't know how to react to either.

Gary was still feeling his way with Evan as the three of them ate dinner together. He was deliberately mischievous, throwing a piece of carrot on the floor and knocking over his milk. Dawn scolded him without much corrective effect, and, at first, Evan seemed indifferent to anything the three-year-old did. When his patience was exhausted, he said a few sharp words to the little boy that made him settle down immediately. They finished their meal in silence, and Evan left, apparently assuming that she would be the one to clean up and load the dishwasher.

When Gary was settled down for the night, without the benefit of any attention from the man she felt sure was his father, Dawn decided she had to call Los Angeles and explain her delay in arriving, but how on earth could she explain a situation like this to her friend Maggie? She didn't even understand it herself.

She dialed Maggie's number, not worrying that Evan

would be billed for a long-distance call to the coast. He'd offered to pay her for staying, and she'd refused, but if he was going to keep her prisoner, let him handle the expenses. Rich or poor, he deserved more than a big phone bill for the way he was treating her.

Maggie's questions were as difficult as Dawn had anticipated. Her friend was burning with curiosity and fired up to do something to rescue her.

"I can call the Iowa state police from here," she suggested.

"No, don't do that. There are reasons why I should stay. For Gary's sake mainly. It just makes me so mad that I'm being forced into it."

"You're not making a whole lot of sense," Maggie said. "You shouldn't let a strange man force you to stay in his house."

"No, I suppose not. Just don't give up on me, friend. How long can it take to check birth records?"

From their experience as social workers, both women knew that the simplest check could hit snags, delays, and holdups, but neither said so.

Maggie talked for a long time, telling her about a possible job opening in her own department, and Dawn finally ended the conversation filled with frustration. Talking with her friend only made her more eager to go; she had to get on with her life. What could she possibly accomplish staying in Evan Crane's house? She didn't tell Maggie that a big new worry was tormenting her: If Evan tried to make love to her, would she have the strength to resist?

"A few days won't matter that much to your friend, will they?"

Evan had entered the room so quietly that he startled her, and she looked at him suspiciously, wondering how much of her phone conversation he had overheard.

"If you want privacy when you make calls, you're welcome to use my office," he offered.

"It's no secret to you that I want to leave for California. Don't you care that I may lose a great job opportunity if I'm too slow getting there?"

"Why not type a résumé and mail it ahead? You're welcome to use my typewriter too."

That his suggestion was so sensible only angered her more. She was beginning to think of him as Mr. Perfect, but he fell far short in one respect. He hadn't even tried to warm up to Gary. In fact, he seemed determined to keep the little boy at arm's length.

"I'll manage my own life, thank you," she said curtly. "You're the one who needs help with human relations."

"Am I supposed to feel insulted and demand to know what you mean by that?"

"I'll tell you whether you ask or not. You could at least be kind to Gary. He's only a young child, and you're so cold, you scare him."

"What you're saying is that I should become attached to him, so I'll take him off your hands whether he's my son or not."

"You twist everything!" she cried out.

They were facing each other, and she felt moisture forming on the palms of her hands. Trying to convince herself that she wasn't afraid of Evan, she forced herself to meet his steady gaze. His lips parted slightly, then shut firmly, making a thin line of them. She had a sudden impulse to trace his mouth with her fingertip, an idea that was definitely unsettling.

"Dawn." He said her name softly, his voice holding a tone she hadn't heard before. In any other man she would have called it passion. She could almost feel his touch again, stirring up sensations that could only confuse and complicate her life.

He moved half a step closer, reaching out to touch her cheek with the backs of two fingers.

36

"Your skin is as soft as I first imagined it," he said, disarming her completely.

She was ready for him to kiss her again, more than ready, straining toward him in expectation and totally forgetting that she despised him. When he stepped away, she hated herself for feeling disappointed. He took her arm lightly and steered her into the family room, but didn't sit beside her on the couch.

"We might as well watch the news," he said. "It's nearly ten."

"That's an hour earlier than we get the evening news at home," she said, glad of a safe, neutral topic like central standard time to allow her to regain her composure.

"Where's home? Pittsburgh?"

"Recently, yes, but my parents live south of there in Washington, Pennsylvania."

"And you're an only child?"

"How did you know?"

"Your reactions tell me that you're used to being unchallenged. Who gets their own way more than only children?"

"You have a great opinion of my maturity."

"How mature are you?"

"If you mean how old, I'm twenty-four."

"That young?"

"I think I'll go to bed."

"I'm only teasing," he said, smiling broadly. "Being ten years older should give me that privilege."

She didn't like the way his smile softened and transformed his face. Or, rather, she liked it too well. The tiny laugh lines showed again by his eyes, and she imagined running her lips over his sharply defined eyebrows, letting his lashes tickle her chin.

Sinking back in an upholstered chair, he draped one long, bare leg over the arm, looking totally at ease. His relaxed pose didn't have a soothing effect on Dawn, however. She felt tense and agitated, hardly able to force herself to sit still. Her hands and feet kept trying to betray her with fidgety little movements, and she felt almost as if she were posting guard over her errant toes and fingers to keep them still.

"You have lovely feet, but why do you keep watching them?" he asked pointedly.

"I'm not."

She tried to stare him down, but he refused to drop his eyes. To save her pride, she pretended to be nonchalant, studying her hand for nonexistent flaws in her manicure.

Sitting upright and putting both feet on the floor, he seemed to signal that their sparring was over.

"You have a right to know what I've done today," he said.

"Rights again?" she joked feebly, but he chose to ignore her comment.

"I called my lawyer, and he's arranging for the investigation, only he'd like to speak to you in person as soon as possible. We'll drive in to see him tomorrow morning. I have a nine o'clock appointment."

"Gary will come with us?"

"No, I have a high school girl coming to baby-sit."

"I knew you could get a sitter if you wanted one."

"You're not here to baby-sit," he said, his good mood turning sour again.

"No, I'm your hostage!"

"It's the price you have to pay for being a busybody do-gooder."

Nothing he could have called her would have been more galling.

"At least I care about Gary!"

She was on her feet and leaving the room when his shou stopped her.

"Damn it, Dawn, let's stop this!"

"I'm not doing anything I need to stop."

"You've already done it. You've created this situation. At least be a good sport about it for a couple of days. You can't expect me to start acting like a super-father to a boy who may have no business being here."

"I have no business being here either. We'll both leave."

"You'll do no such thing, not until I'm ready to have you go."

"That time can't come quickly enough."

"Can't it?"

He grabbed her shoulders and forced her to look at him.

"Just be sure of one thing. It's no picnic for me having you here."

She escaped to her room, intending to have a good old-fashioned bawl, but crying wasn't adequate to cope with the way she felt. Her whole future hinged on getting to California as quickly as possible, yet knowing Evan wanted to be rid of her was hard for her ego to handle. She'd always thought the plots in romantic novels where the heroines fell in love with their captors were nonsense; in real life the situation would be ludicrous. If she started thinking about Evan that way, it would be a catastrophe.

He was bossy, overbearing, smug, and egotistical. In fact, if she wanted to play the old alphabet game, she could find a derogatory word to describe him for every letter. She tried it, having no trouble with A, B, or C. Arrogant, beastly, and cocky. Thinking ahead to the hard letters, she decided on quick-tempered for Q and vicious for V, but all she could think of for X was X-rated. Thinking that way wouldn't do at all. Unless she could bring herself to consider Mr. Evan Crane totally asexual, even undesirable, these were going to be the longest days of her life.

This night she was much more cautious when she crept across the hall to check on Gary, but her stealth was unnecessary. The little boy was alone in the room, looking lonesome and vulnerable in the oversize bed.

"Oh, Gary," she whispered, "what have I gotten both of us into? If only you were mine to love the way you should be loved!"

CHAPTER THREE

Evan had done a thorough job of unloading Dawn's luggage and other possessions from her car. Everything she'd considered necessary to begin her new life in California was somewhere in the bedroom, and she was only thankful she'd decided to store most of her books and mementoes at her parents' house temporarily. When it came to unpacking, she was torn between the need to have things where she could find them and a reluctance to settle into the room that belonged to Evan Crane. Putting all her clothes in the closet and drawers seemed to be a sign of surrender, so she compromised, trying to pick out only the most essential items and leaving the rest in her suitcases and boxes. The result, of course, was that everything she needed was hidden away somewhere, including the shoes and the carved wooden bracelet she wanted to wear with her lemon-yellow halter dress.

The impatient knock on her door only threw her into a frenzy.

"Dawn, we have to leave," Evan said, his attempt to mask his impatience not very successful.

"I'm nearly ready."

She decided to forget about the bracelet, but a bit of smudged mascara delayed her anyway. When she hurried into the family room to tell Evan she was ready, she was thoroughly disgusted with herself. She'd primped like a schoolgirl to get ready for a business meeting with Evan

Crane and his lawyer, as if either of them cared whether she came in an evening gown or a pair of farmer's overalls. As it was, she felt rather unbusinesslike; the continuing heat had made her decide on her coolest, barest summer cotton. Her decision to wear it had nothing to do with the fact that it made her waist look tiny and her bustline full and provocative. Evan's lawyer probably had snowy hair and seven grandchildren, and she wouldn't consider dressing to please her jailer.

Evan certainly didn't fit anyone's image of a working farmer when he courteously handed her into the plush gray interior of his Lincoln. Wearing a summer suit expertly tailored in a textured off-white fabric, he moved like an athlete and looked like a highly placed executive.

Dawn knew they were going to Des Moines, since she'd read the note he'd left for the sitter, but she didn't know what he would expect of her when they got there.

"Why are we driving all the way to Des Moines to see a lawyer?" she asked.

"That's where his office is. It's only an hour's drive."

"I suppose you played football with your attorney too?"

"No, I knew him in college."

"College?"

"Don't seem surprised. We rural rubes go to school too. Iowa State is one of the best universities in the world for agriculture, among other things."

"Is that what you studied? Farming?"

"Argicultural management. My masters is in finance."

Learning that his education equalled hers didn't put her more at ease. In fact, she felt as though she'd lost an advantage, although she'd never mentioned to him that she had her masters in social work.

They traveled over vast expanses of flatland, varied by some pleasantly rolling land, but the view was one of endless fields, green with either corn or soybeans. Dawn felt a tinge of homesickness for the rockier hills of Pennsylvania, but there was an aura of fertility and richness about the land that kept it from becoming monotonous.

Evan was quiet, answering her questions pleasantly enough, but taking no initiative in carrying on a conversation. He drove with total concentration, but was content to hold his powerful car to the legal speed limit.

Entering the network of expressways that skirted Des Moines was like coming upon any large city. Its individuality was lost in the monotony of the transportation system, but the golden dome of the state capitol building did evoke her admiration. Was the gold symbolic of the perishable gold of Iowa's fields?

They parked with relative ease near the multistoried building that was their destination, and Evan picked that time to coach Dawn for their appointment.

"Tell Cliff Harding everything you can possibly remember about Sheila, no matter how insignificant it seems. See if you can think of the names of any of her close friends, if she has any. Let Cliff decide what's important and what isn't."

"You don't need to prompt me," she said crossly.

"Of course, you're the lady who rearranges lives. You can handle yourself in any situation, can't you?"

The undercurrent of criticism stung more than his comment, knowing as she did what situation he meant, but she wouldn't give him the satisfaction of an answer. Tilting her head up rather more than was necessary, she got out of the car and flounced off. Unfortunately she went in the wrong direction, and it didn't do her self-esteem any good when he laughingly retrieved her and took her arm to steer her in the right direction.

Cliff Harding looked younger than Evan, even though they had been classmates; with black hair, dark brown eyes, and a stocky, muscular build, he was considerably shorter than Evan and very much his opposite in many ways. The men greeted each other cordially, then, flatteringly, Cliff turned the full impact of his charm on Dawn. Even though she knew his compliments were overly flowery and less than sincere, she rather enjoyed them, and when Evan let her see a tiny trace of irritation, she decided to flirt with the attorney for all she was worth.

"Let's get on with this, shall we?" Evan asked just as Cliff was telling Dawn how fetching her dress was.

Nothing much came of the interview as far as Dawn could tell. She'd already told Evan all she knew about Sheila, and Chicago remained the only lead they had on the birth of Gary. Both men seemed interested in her evaluation of Sheila as a mother, and the conversation got into topics like unchanged diapers and unsuitable baby-sitters. It made Dawn wonder why they were so interested in evidence that Sheila was an unfit mother, but neither man seemed inclined to explain. After what seemed like an unnecessarily long interview, Evan became restless, getting up from his chair and pacing while Cliff continued talking to Dawn.

"She's told you all she knows," Evan said, making no secret of his eagerness to leave. "We have to go. I need to stop at the John Deere dealer to check on a part on the way home."

"That sounds dull for Dawn," Cliff said. "Let her stay here with me, and we'll meet you for lunch. I have to run over to the capitol to see one of the legislators, and I'm sure she'd rather see the grand old building than a tractor showroom. You pick the restaurant, and we'll meet you there."

"Afraid that's not very convenient today, Cliff," Evan said. "We'll be going now. Thanks for handling this the right way, and be sure to keep me posted."

Dawn wasn't reluctant to leave the attorney's office; his aggressive flirting and the wedding ring on his finger weren't a combination she admired, but it hadn't done her mood a bit of harm to see that Evan was mildly displeased.

44

"Why are you still single?" he asked as soon as they were inside his car.

"That's my business!"

"Oh? According to your rules, you can barge into my life, hand me a kid who may or may not be my son, and disappear, but I can't ask you a simple question?"

"My personal life has nothing to do with you."

Why did she feel as though she were skating on thin ice?

"What about my personal life? You didn't hesitate to ask me if I could have impregnated my wife."

"I certainly never put it that way! Talking with you is impossible."

"Then give me a straight answer to my question. I know you're not single because you've lacked opportunities. Cliff Harding is a connoisseur; he only comes on to real winners."

"I imagine his wife appreciates that."

"I wouldn't know. Now, why aren't you married?" he asked again, raising one eyebrow.

"I have my career," she said primly.

"I already know that. Isn't there room in your life for a husband, a home, kids, all the things women are supposed to want?"

He'd triggered her indignation, but she fought the urge to lash out at him, knowing that he was playing a game with her. A show of anger would make her the loser.

"Of course, all us old-fashioned girls are pining for a big strong husband, a freshly starched apron, and a row of noses to wipe."

"Okay," he said, laughing softly, "I did come on like a chauvinist. I apologize, but you really don't make it very easy."

His gentle tone appealed to her where forcefulness wouldn't have, and she answered slowly, trying to be honest without sounding like a militant for the women's movement.

"I thought about marrying once, but it meant giving up any possibility of a career to live in a lonely, isolated place. I couldn't face having nothing to do for months, maybe years, on end."

"Also you didn't love the guy enough?"

"I suppose that's true," she said, admitting it to herself as much as to him.

Evan's business with the farm equipment dealer took only a few minutes, but Dawn certainly wouldn't have been bored if it'd taken an hour. She walked among the giant machines on display outside, feeling like one of Gulliver's Lilliputians beside massive tractor wheels and machinery designed to work six or eight rows of corn at a time. Her wanderings added a new dimension to her understanding of Evan: Apparently it took a big man to be fully in control of the beasts of modern food production.

"It looks like I'll have to feed you," he said when he rejoined her, very effectively destroying all her romantic fantasies about strong men of the soil.

"Only if you're hungry yourself," she snapped.

Evan left the expressway and followed a maze of corn-lined country roads that completely defeated Dawn's imperfect sense of direction. When he did stop, they were in a town so small it didn't seem to have a name. The restaurant he chose was named appropriately, if not imaginatively, Fine Food Café.

"I could have been wining and dining with Cliff in Des Moines," she pointed out.

"Not like you can here."

Evan insisted on ordering for her in the surprisingly crowded little restaurant. Workingmen for miles around seemed to gather there for lunch, or dinner, as the menu called it. They both had Iowa pork chops, great slabs of meat thicker than three regular chops and baked to fork-cutting tenderness in tangy sauce. With the meal came spinach salad, a huge baked potato smothered in sour cream, a mound of squash swimming in butter, and large mugs of coffee. All this came to them after Evan said, "We'll have the pork chops."

What was even nicer than the meal was the fact that they were talking like two ordinary people who enjoyed each other's company. They exchanged anecdotes about their families, found they shared a passion for golf, and agreed that valuable Indian archeological sites were in danger of being obliterated. They also managed to avoid any mention of Gary, Sheila, or California. All in all, it was an amazingly pleasant interlude.

"Back to work," he said regretfully, and Dawn felt the same reluctance to leave the plain little restaurant with its 1940s hodgepodge of tables and plastic-backed chairs.

Evan was besieged with messages that the baby-sitter had carefully written out for him, and Gary demanded Dawn's attention forcefully as soon as they returned. The outing was over, but Dawn had discovered one thing— Evan Crane was a person she could learn to like a great deal. He could be witty, entertaining, and stimulating. It was beginning to seem a shame that she'd never see him again after she left Iowa, but remembering that he could also be threatening, domineering, and sexually aggressive, she knew the sooner she left, the better.

Lunch had been so filling and so fattening that Dawn fixed a hotdog for Gary and just a salad for herself for dinner. They ate alone in the kitchen, but both of them had one eye on the door, anticipating Evan's return. He didn't come.

The next day Mrs. Winsch was scheduled to come to Evan's, so, illogically, Dawn spent the early evening cleaning for the cleaning woman. She followed the trail left by Gary's active play, picking up toys and wiping fingerprints from walls and tables. He was having a wonderful time without Sheila's repressive control, but many of his play habits reflected her neglect. Gary was a cheerful, willing

47

learner; Dawn was sure that he'd improve rapidly if some-one cared enough to teach him. The only question was, who would spend their days helping him grow up? Even after she left, Evan was far too involved in the manage-ment of his unusually large farm to be much of a parent. Possibly Mrs. Winsch could be persuaded that she was needed here full time, or maybe Evan knew a woman who would be glad to fill the role if he asked her. That was a new thought, and not a pleasant solution, although Dawn hated to admit to herself that the possibility of Evan hav-ing a love life was far from agreeable.

After escaping the heat by playing inside all day, Gary was rowdy and clammering to go outside. Being allowed to run free outside was such a delight to him that Dawn couldn't resist his plea. After spraying both of them with a liberal amount of insect repellent, she spent the rest of Gary's time before bed playing ball and tag with him in the yard. She was ready for bed herself by the time they went inside, but Gary was overly stimulated. Not even a warm bath and a long story calmed him enough to get him to sleep. Evan found them together in Gary's room, with the little rascal jumping up and down on his bed and trying to evade Dawn at the same time.

"Well, you really have things under control," he said, surveying the chaotic scene from the doorway.

The sophisticated man in the off-white suit had become transformed, and Evan looked grubby and weary in faded jeans and a well-worn knit shirt bleached to a pale gray. Gary plopped down on his pajama-clad bottom and eyed Evan warily.

"Young man, I'm going to take a shower. When I'm done, you'd better be asleep."

A sobered child let himself be tucked into bed, but, grateful as she was to have him settled, Dawn was uneasy about Gary's reaction to Evan. Unused to men, except for Sheila's dates who only popped in and out of his life, Gary seemed to be afraid of him. Would Evan's harshness soften once he was sure of Gary's parentage? It was something they had to discuss. Not even for the sake of her own career would she leave Gary in a home where he would feel intimidated and unloved.

Evan's system for evening meals was simple. Mrs. Winsch prepared several meals and froze individual portions that he could heat in the microwave when his long hours allowed him to have dinner. When she heard him in the kitchen, Dawn offered to help, but there was little to do. She fixed a salad and poured a glass of milk; the rest was done. Evan Crane didn't need a full-time woman to order his life.

Sitting across from each other as he ate, they were each very aware of the other, but there was none of the pleasant small talk they'd enjoyed at their noon meal.

"You look tired," she ventured to say.

"Beat."

When he finished, he did smile warmly, unintentionally giving her a go-ahead signal to bring up Gary.

"Can we talk?" she asked with some nervousness.

"Let's go out to the patio."

She followed him to the screened area, choosing to sit on the old-fashioned glider. A metal relic from the 1930s, it was the only piece that didn't match the sturdy, modern, redwood patio furniture, although new, matching cushions had replaced the original ones. Evan joined her there, and for a while they moved back and forth, both pairs of legs contributing to the gentle rhythm of movement.

"What's our topic of conversation?" he asked.

"Gary."

"Ah."

"And you."

"Of course."

"I think he's scared of you, Evan."

"He'd better be, if he intends to use his bed as a trampoline."

"He's been allowed to grow up without much guidance, I know, but he's an agreeable little boy. He was quick to learn what irritated Sheila."

"I'm sure I'd rather not know what that was."

"Anything that made demands on her," Dawn said bitterly. "That's just the point. He was a little afraid of her, I'm sure. He doesn't need more fear. He needs to trust people because he knows they care about him."

"We're back to that, then."

"Evan, all I'm asking is that you be gentle with him. He hasn't had a very good start in life, you know."

"Regardless of what you think, I do know that. But we don't know if I'm his father yet, do we?"

"No, but—"

"No buts. I see your drift, and I'll try not to be an ogre. That doesn't mean Gary can behave like a savage and get away with it though. If you can't control him while you're here, I won't promise not to step in."

"But do it kindly," she begged.

He smiled in spite of himself. "Okay, kindly it is, but that doesn't rule out a pat on the behind if he's tearing the place apart."

His hand slipped from the back of the glider to her shoulder and gently kneaded it.

"I'll bet when you were a kid you brought home birds with broken wings and snakes with broken tails," he teased softly.

"Well, birds, anyway," she admitted, her mind on his hand, not his words.

He moved closer, his arm totally enveloping her shoulder. Even though his legs kept up the slow rocking of the glider, she felt frozen stiff. His touch was a combination of pleasure and threat, and she didn't know how to read it. Almost against her will, she shifted her position so she

50

could see him better, but his face was hidden in shadow. The light filtered through the sliding doors from the family room, but it failed to reach their corner of the patio.

"Dawn," he whispered, his face moving closer to hers.

She was ready, even yearning for his kiss, but he backed away suddenly and stopped.

"I'd b-better go in," she stammered.

"No."

He caught her as she moved to stand, sending her off-balance and steadying her in his arms. His kiss was greedy, too quick and too sensual to overcome all the restraints she imposed on herself. Her reaction was instinctive, pushing against his chest and twisting to free herself.

"I'm sorry." He backed away as abruptly as he'd begun, turning his back and walking toward the family-room door.

"Maybe I should let you go," he said without turning toward her.

She ran after him, catching at his shirt to make him stop.

"Don't," he said.

She pulled her hand away as if he'd slapped it, her struggle for self-control only half won.

"Evan, I didn't mean to push you away. I just wasn't ready—"

"For this?"

Pulling her close, he peppered her upturned face with tiny, nipping kisses, then found her parted lips with his. His cheek, pressed against her nostrils, was slightly scented with spicy soap, and the first trace of his beard felt slightly abrasive on her chin. She was all sensation, electrified by the contact wherever their bodies touched.

His face softened with passion. He lifted her against his chest, freeing her lips but capturing her legs under the knees.

"Evan, you can't lift me—"

He silenced her with a demanding kiss, then moved down the hallway, carrying her weight easily against his torso.

"Put me down, Evan!"

"I will."

He kicked open the door of his bedroom and eased her down on his king-size bed. She watched in a daze as he closed the door, pushing the handle to lock it, then pulling his shirt off before he approached her again.

His kisses built up in intensity, their intent seeming to draw out her very essence, and she felt her lifelong habit of control and deliberation slipping away. Everything seemed to be happening to someone else.

Nothing he did betrayed his own eagerness; slowly and carefully removing her soft knit shirt, caressing and kissing every inch of exposed skin on her shoulders and neck, he finally cupped one breast in his hand and used the other to unclasp her bra.

"We have to talk, Evan," she insisted, trying to turn off the sensations that were clouding her judgment.

"Let your body talk for you, darling. Don't ignore the message it's sending you."

"Evan, has there been anyone since your wife?"

His groan came from deep in his throat.

"Dawn, don't tell me you want to take my case history now!"

He rolled over on his back, taking her with him. Holding her on his chest, he wrapped his legs around her squirming limbs and held her quietly until her eyes focused on his.

"This isn't going the way it should," Dawn said, dropping her forehead against his chin to avoid his eyes, but closing her own to avoid studying the whorls of golden-tipped hair on his chest.

"It seems to be moving along in the normal way," he said, smiling in spite of his letdown. "I'd have guessed I

52

have a lot more experience than you to base my analysis on."

"That's a low blow," she said, able now to roll to his side.

"I want you, Dawn." His voice was husky as he leaned over her again, lightly touching her lips with his.

The moment she began to respond to his kiss, Evan imprisoned her legs with one of his own. Evan's hard length pressed against her, head to toe, unnerving her as she struggled with him and herself.

For a moment she was winning, her freed hand pushing desperately at his chest, but his strength wasn't the weapon she really feared. Pinning her on her back, he began his assault with melting tenderness. A tiny lick on her nose, a feathery kiss on her ear lobe, his breath warm on her eyelid—these were the forays that quieted her doubts.

Encouraged by her tiny gasp of pleasure when his moist tongue touched her breast, he began his seduction in earnest, whispering the commands of lovemaking, directing her without seeming to demand. Even his kiss on her shoulder produced ripples of pleasure, and the only struggle now was in her mind. She had the sensation that she was drowning, losing control of her own identity. It was a delicious and a frightening sensation; part of her wanted every possible pleasure Evan was offering. The other part cautioned her to remember that there was more to her life than casual sex with a man whose personality clashed impossibly with hers.

Removing the rest of her clothing while she was still embroiled in sensations, he fondled her gently, giving her a chance to realize that nothing he intended would be abrupt or hurtful.

"It can't be all taking," he said softly. "You have to give too."

He guided her unresisting hand until she was exploring

on her own the mat of hair that thinned over his navel and disappeared below his waistband.

Shuddering under her touch, he moved aside to remove the rest of his clothing, becoming too impatient now to wait for her to do it.

As he hovered over her, she felt genuine, blinding panic for the first time in her life.

"I want you, Dawn," he murmured insistently. "It's been so long."

His words were like a cold shower on her emotions. Of course, he wanted sex; he must not have a convenient partner and he was a healthy, vibrant male. But sex wasn't a gift she could hand out casually to a man she'd just met, a man who would very soon pass out of her life forever. Robbed of the sense of specialness, Dawn retaliated in the only way she knew—she resisted him.

"No, Evan," she cried, throwing her body to the side to evade his fresh embrace.

"Dawn." There was surprise and hurt in his voice as he tried to pull her back into his arms. "Why are you doing this now?"

She didn't know why, but she groped for excuses.

"I'm not ready for this. We shouldn't do this. I might get pregnant."

"I won't force you," he said wearily, letting her go and sitting on the far edge of the bed with his back toward her, "and I won't play games."

The size of his bed thwarted any possibility of a dignified exit. She crawled to the opposite side, away from him, still far from being in control. Her bra was hanging on the edge, and she couldn't find her shirt.

"I don't know what you want," she cried out on the verge of tears.

"I couldn't make it much plainer."

"Oh, I know, you want me that way, Evan, but things have to be spelled out for me. I can't lose control of my

own life. I have plans, aspirations. I can't throw everything away just to . . . to . . ."

"To make love."

"Yes—no."

He stood and looked at her with partially hooded eyes,
but, trying to avoid seeing his body, she missed the expression on his face.

"I may not sleep very well tonight, Dawn, but I sure as
hell am going to try. Unless you intend to join me, you'd
better get out."

"You have no right to sound so bitter," she cried out.

"No? Do you think it's fun being led on by a tease?"

"I'm not a tease!" His accusation stung her. "You're
keeping me prisoner here. You have no right to start
something like this."

"I'm sick of hearing that word *right!* You should talk
about taking advantage!" he stormed, going to his closet
and yanking out a robe. "You weren't invited here to
destroy my peace of mind. I don't need you or a kid. It
was rough going after Peg left, but I've ordered my life so
I don't need anyone. Remember that next time you feel
amorous, and find someone else to watch you wiggle your
butt."

"I do not wiggle!"

The look he gave her as she finally found her shirt was
so black, she started to leave without putting it on.

"I want my car keys," she demanded from the doorway.

"Did your plan to get them prove too hazardous? No
way." There was iron stubbornness in his voice. "You got
yourself into this, and you're staying right here until it's
resolved. It can't be too soon for me, but you won't
manipulate me the way you do your welfare clients."

"What a rotten, despicable thing to say."

"The truth sometimes is. Get out of my room."

Running from his room into hers, she felt her hot tears
burn her cheeks. Great, heaving sobs shook her whole

55

body as she buried her face in her pillow, even in her misery trying to stifle her sounds so Evan wouldn't know how badly he had shaken her.

Damn him! She did want him! She wanted to touch him and hold him; she yearned to mold her body to his, to revel in his masculinity, to receive the full impact of his love-making. She felt just as empty and frustrated as he must feel, but things between them couldn't be casual and meaningless. To be in his bed simply because it was a pleasant convenience was intolerable, but the alternative was impossible. Any kind of commitment between them was unthinkable. His life was orderly, arranged according to a pattern that wouldn't be altered to accommodate her needs. Her future was elsewhere, and he'd never suggested that it wasn't.

"Damn you, Evan Crane!" she said aloud, reaching for a wad of tissues to mop her dripping face. "The worst thing you've done is make me care about you."

She hoped he'd twist and turn all night, tormented by his own ill-advised advances. If she had encouraged him, she bitterly regretted it, but she would let him suffer mightily for trying to take advantage of her when she was nothing to him but a convenience.

Afraid to risk using the connecting bathroom, she crept out to the half-bath by the kitchen and inundated her face with the chill water that came from the farm's deep well. She was going back to her room, when a sobbing sound arrested her movement.

Entering Gary's room, she found him sitting up in bed, crying robustly.

"Honey, what's the matter?" she asked, gathering him into her arms and blotting his tears with one of the tissues she'd brought to catch any stray tears of her own.

It was futile to question the crying child, so she held him until he was quiet.

"Dawn, stay," he said brokenly.

"Everything's fine," she assured him softly.

"Stay," he insisted again.

Throwing textbook advice to the wind, she crawled in beside him, taking comfort from the small hand that wouldn't loosen its grip on hers.

Later, much later, a quiet figure stood in the doorway, watching the two of them sleep.

CHAPTER FOUR

Lying in bed long after she awoke the next morning, Dawn strained to hear sounds of Evan's leaving and, at the same time, kept still herself so she wouldn't wake Gary. The little boy was quiet in his sleep, as he wasn't at any other time, and his face beside her on the pillow was angelic. She would have enjoyed just watching him sleep if another, more disturbing image hadn't intruded. How close she had come to waking up beside Evan! Instead of Gary's fine, almost colorless baby hair so close it nearly tickled her cheek, it could have been Evan's thicker, tawny hair. A sudden spasm of longing ran down her spine, and she struggled to hold back tears. How could she want someone so intensely when he was so wrong for her?

Belatedly she remembered that it was Mrs. Winsch's day to come. Unaccustomed as she was to having domestic help, she couldn't permit herself to lie in bed while the woman did enough work for three people. Her watch was in her room, and there was no clock in Gary's room, so she had to get up to see what time it was. The house seemed completely quiet, so she chanced making a run for her door, hoping against hope that Evan really had left the house.

It was the worst possible timing. She nearly collided with him coming down the hallway from his room. He stopped almost on top of her and made a dignified retreat impossible. In her pink nylon shorty pajamas Dawn felt

58

vulnerable and exposed, and without thinking she crossed her arms over her chest.

"Good morning."

The calm indifference in his voice was chilling; either he was masterfully in control of his emotions or he really didn't care that she had ended their encounter so abruptly the night before.

"Good morning," she mumbled, reaching for the knob of her door without meeting his eyes.

"Is Gary awake?" He wouldn't let her get by him so easily.

"Not yet."

"Well, let him sleep a little longer, but have him fed and dressed by eight thirty. I'm going to show the two of you around the place before it gets too hot."

Even if she could have thought of an argument against his offer, he didn't give her a chance to voice it. He left her standing alone in the hallway, as though he hadn't the slightest doubt that she'd follow his directions. How could he be so totally in control, when she felt like disintegrating? He was inhuman! Any normal man would have pouted or made nasty remarks or refused to talk to her after the way she'd cut off their lovemaking. Did he care so little that he'd put it out of his mind already?

A contrary streak in Dawn urged her to keep Evan waiting, if only to show him that he had no authority over her, but common sense won out. Gary was fed and dressed, ready to go promptly at eight thirty. Armed with a suitable series of excuses, Dawn was determined not to go herself. She'd seen quite enough of Iowa already, and the prospect of being with Evan for any amount of time was unnerving.

"Everyone ready?" Evan called heartily on his way through the kitchen.

"Gary's ready, but I'm not going," Dawn answered, deliberately calling to him from the family room and banking on Mrs. Winsch's presence to keep him from insisting.

Walking into the room, he directed all his attention to Gary, talking to him in a friendly, cheerful way.

"Say, where's your cowboy hat, friend? Better go find it. That sun gets pretty hot."

All he said to Dawn was "You're going."

"You cannot order me around," she whispered, furious.

"You're the one who wants me to be nice to Gary. I have eighty different jobs I should be doing, but here I am. Are the two of you coming with me or is the trip off?"

"That's blackmail!"

"Call it what you like."

Gary bounded into the room, his wariness of Evan pushed aside by the prospect of riding in a truck. His toy truck, a gift from Dawn the previous Christmas, was his favorite possession, and his main source of entertainment on their trip west had been the trucks that passed them on the highways. When they went outside, his excitement at being so close to the real thing was contagious, and Evan let him investigate the wheels and bumpers of the farm's pickup truck at his leisure, then lifted him into the back.

"He can't ride back there alone," Dawn pointed out, starting to climb up to join him.

"It's too hot and dusty for either of you to ride in back. Just let him play there a few minutes so he knows what it's like."

Evan lifted her from the fender to the ground, putting his hands on her waist and handling her as though she were as light as Gary.

"Please, don't do that," she said stiffly.

He dropped his hands to his sides, his expression totally unreadable.

"I won't force myself on you," he said harshly. "I misread your interest last night, but you can be sure it won't happen again."

He turned away from her, giving all his attention to Gary, who had just about lost interest in his high perch on the bed of the unmoving truck.

Dawn held Gary on her lap in the cab of the truck, sitting as close to the window as possible but still conscious of every move Evan made. His hands gripped the wheel tighter than necessary, she could tell, but that was the only sign that he was disturbed too. Even though she tried not to look in his direction, she was aware of his thigh, his comfortably worn jeans failing to hide the muscular molding.

"Know what we're going to see, Gary?" he asked. "I'll give you a hint. It's an animal."

"Dog," Gary guessed enthusiastically.

"Wrong. Guess again."

They worked their way through a barnyard's worth of possibilities and finally got to the pig. Holding the pint-size bundle of eagerness on her lap was like containing a little cyclone, and Dawn hoped the ride was a short one. She was going to get some black-and-blue marks out of this excursion.

"Gary, sit still," she commanded more crossly than she'd intended.

Surprisingly he obeyed, startled at her unusual sharpness, but Evan was no help at all. He grinned and winked at Gary, as if to say "We have to humor her; she's a girl."

The house where Evan stopped was much more in keeping with Dawn's notion of a farm home. Built on a small hill, it rose straight up for three stories, seemingly much too high for its narrow width. The siding was painted gray, but at first glance it looked like weather-beaten wood, as though the house had been allowed to age naturally for many generations.

"This looks more like a farmhouse," Dawn said, forgetting for a moment the tension that had been building between them.

Evan laughed softly and pulled Gary off her lap.

"This is my family's second house," he said.

"Second house?"

"My great-grandfather built it at the end of the last century, when his family got too big for the original homestead. He had thirteen children, but my grandfather was the only male to survive World War One and the influenza epidemic."

"How long has your family been here?" Dawn asked, intrigued in spite of her growing shyness with Evan.

"I'm the fifth generation. My great-great-grandfather was a Civil War veteran. He brought his family here in a covered wagon and homesteaded one hundred fifty-five acres. It's been traditional for every generation to add some acreage. The family's been lucky in that we were able to keep growing. Inheritance taxes make it rougher all the time."

"So Gary will be the sixth generation," Dawn said, deliberately testing his reaction.

Instantly his face became a closed mask, and his only comment was "Maybe."

He waited with Gary's hand in his as she scrambled down from the high truck seat, then started walking toward a barn that looked like an old-fashioned one.

"Who lives here now?" Dawn asked, wondering if Evan had some relatives he hadn't mentioned, relatives who might help with Gary.

"My foreman, Dewey Clatt, and his wife, Betty. They have two kids in their teens, but they're all out helping the detasseling crews. That's where I should be," he added dryly, wanting her to know that he was being inconvenienced.

Dawn bit back the sarcastic comment she wanted to make; it was very important that Gary get to know his father, and this was the first time Evan had shown any interest in him.

The odor in the barn was much too pungent for Dawn's comfort, but she followed the two of them into the dusky interior anyway, not wanting to call attention to her city-girl fastidiousness.

Here was the farm she had promised Gary, and he was delighted. Skittish barn cats hissed at them, but kept their distance, and a spotted brown and white horse with huge, soulful eyes invited petting. Evan even pulled a sugar cube from his pocket and showed Gary how to offer it, assuring him that the horse's big teeth wouldn't hurt him, although the boy didn't show the slightest fear of the animal.

The lords of the barn were also the source of the burning in Dawn's nostrils, she soon discovered, as they viewed the massive swine. Each pig seemed larger than the last—monuments of living flesh that seemed obscene to Dawn, whose only contact with the world of livestock had been an occasional country fair.

Gary didn't seem to share Dawn's reservations, however, listening avidly to everything Evan told him. She heard enough to realize that hog-raising was a sideline for the foreman, but that Evan wasn't involved in it himself. The culmination of the trip through the barn was Gary's excitement over a litter of baby pigs still small enough for them to be pets. Dawn left the barn before the two males; they could explore that aspect of farming without any encouragement from her.

"Come on," Evan finally called to her. "We'll go out to a field where they're working."

Dawn loved growing things, and the green fields appealed to her much more than the confines of the barn. Seeing animals stuffed to provide meat was enough to make her think of being a vegetarian, but the sheer vastness of the cornfields was awe-inspiring.

Except for a larger truck parked beside the gravel road, there was no immediate evidence that anyone was working in the field Evan brought them to, but the sense of isolation was deceptive. Several dozen people were walking down rows of corn, unseen except when they finished a row at the end near the road.

Dawn met Betty Clatt, a thin, cheerful woman with graying hair who manned large containers of lemonade and cold water for the workers. Apparently Evan hadn't mentioned either Gary or Dawn to his foreman's wife, because the woman's friendliness was fired by a great deal of curiosity.

Gary darted up and down between the closest two rows, enjoying the challenge of running on the rough earth, but when he ducked through the stalks and out of sight, Evan sped after him immediately. He carried him back, put him down, and lectured him sternly about staying in sight.

"You have to watch the little ones in the fields," Betty Clatt explained to Dawn. "It's so easy for them to get lost and darn near impossible to find them if they wander far."

"Last summer a kid about Gary's size nearly died," Evan said, holding on to the small, wiggling hand.

"Nearly two thousand people searched for three days," Betty continued, obviously loving to tell a good story. "The newspapers said he must have been scared and hid or something, but he was out there alone for nearly three days, and they found him still alive."

"It's true," Evan added, seeming to sense Dawn's skepticism, "but the unbelievable part was that they found him alive, not that he was lost."

"Kids sure do have to be watched around a farm," Betty said. "Like those two boys who fell into a silo and died."

Guessing that Betty's store of tragic stories was a large one, Dawn interrupted with a question, wondering how they'd finally managed to find the child missing in the cornfields.

"Oh, they tried everything," Betty assured her. "Bloodhounds and airplanes and row-by-row search teams.

Psychics called from all over the country. One thought the child was wedged in someplace, I remember, and it was a psychic who said he was still alive on the third day. That's why a neighbor went out to look one more time in his field, and he was the one who found him. Strange, how those psychics know sometimes. My aunt always said she knew when my uncle was going to pass on."

Evan ended their visit rather abruptly. Dawn would have liked to talk longer with Betty Clatt, not because she was interested in tragedies and psychics, but because she sensed the other woman's need for companionship. Rural women must cherish their time spent just visiting, Dawn decided, and the idea interested her, as did anything concerning people's adjustment to their life-styles. Working mostly with other women, she had never felt deprived of female companionship, but it could be very different on a farm. She wondered if the quality of friendship between women improved when the opportunities lessened. It was a thought that she considered all the way back to the house.

Evan stayed at the house only long enough for Mrs. Winsch to fix him a sack lunch and a thermos of coffee. Then he left, telling Dawn not to expect him for dinner. After a morning of exploring the farm, she was as sleepy as Gary, and they both took long naps in the afternoon.

The rest of the day went slowly, even though Gary kept her more than busy. Stimulated by so many new sights and sounds, his curiosity was seemingly endless. Every corner, every object, every drawer, had to be examined, explored, and explained. She began to realize why the mothers who came to the welfare office often looked harried and hounded.

She didn't begrudge Gary her attention or her affection, but her mind wasn't with him. When he discovered a pipe stand with tobacco in the humidor attached to it that he nearly succeeded in tasting, Dawn wondered how Evan would look smoking a pipe and whether it would have a spicy outdoor scent or smell like burning garbage.

Gary pulled some books from a shelf, and Dawn discovered Evan's yearbook from high school. There he was on the football team, by far the most handsome player in spite of having his hair cut much shorter than now. She counted seven pictures of him in different activities, not including his formal senior portrait reproduced with the prediction that he was "worthy and sure of success."

She slammed the book so hard that Gary forgot his truck and came over to her. How could she be moaning over a man the way a high school sophomore would? Fortunately all of Evan's books were arranged by height, so she could replace the yearbook correctly. He'd never know she was studying it; she didn't know herself why she should be interested in it, or why her interest made her so uneasy.

Sitting alone on the patio after Gary was in bed, she watched the fireflies making erratic flights in the dark and heard the noisemakers of the night, the energetic crickets with their ancient calls, and the nameless hummers and whizzers. A light was showing in the barn, but it wasn't a welcoming beacon for her. She was very much alone; her loneliness was almost tangible.

With a tinge of guilt she wondered what her parents were doing. Naturally they'd been a little apprehensive when they learned that their only child was going so far from home, but their confidence in her decision fortified her. Her promised call to them on her arrival would be late in coming, so she decided this was as good a time as any to tell them she was delayed in Iowa. Remembering her friend Maggie's offer to call the state police from California, she decided to spare her parents most of the details. If her father heard that a strange man was forcing her to stay in his house, he'd have friends from the Air Force

66

Reserve checking on her within the hour. His years in the service had given him a network of acquaintances world-wide, and he wouldn't hesitate to send rescuers if he even suspected she was in trouble.

This was the first time she'd been in Evan's office, the room beyond his bedroom at the end of the house, and being there reminded her that she hadn't started a résumé, even though it would be a very good idea to do so. If she wanted to concentrate on it, this was certainly a room designed for work. A huge desk with an uncluttered top showed that Evan was as orderly in his work habits as he was in everything else, and a multitude of file cabinets reinforced this. The oversize swivel chair covered in red leather was the sole item that suggested any consideration for comfort, and the walls held only degrees and awards, nothing as personal as photographs.

Feeling more than a little depressed, Dawn dialed direct and caught her parents playing gin rummy with their neighbors. The presence of friends limited her father's questions somewhat, and when Dawn hung up, she left them with the impression that she was doing a favor for a friend. The strain of being casual for their benefit made her feel the beginning twinge of a headache, but she was too restless to go to bed. The patio was the only place that appealed to her.

Coming from the brightly lit family room to the dark patio, Dawn had to let her eyes adjust before she realized that someone was there. It took her another moment to see Evan asleep on one of the lounge chairs.

Feeling like an intruder, she almost retreated to her room, but her need to be near him for just a little while stopped her. Moving as quietly as possible on the rush matting, she walked in front of him and stood studying his relaxed face in the dim light. A wave of intense tenderness washed over her, and some unseen force made her draw even closer, until she was leaning over him, her face only inches from his.

Without thinking of the consequences, she brushed her lips with feathery lightness against his brow, then touched his windblown hair with the tip of one finger. When these gentle gestures didn't wake him, she pressed her luck just a bit too far.

Her lips grazed the corner of his eye where his tiny laugh lines made a barely perceptible pattern, and he reacted instantly, pulling her down against him and bumping her hip on the arm of the lounger.

"Ow," she cried out.

"Are you hurt?" he asked, holding her on his lap without chance of escape.

"You pulled me against the wooden arm," she accused him, rubbing what was sure to be a noticeable bruise.

"Sorry, it was unintentional. You startled me awake. What were you doing?"

"I thought a mosquito landed on your face."

"So you were going to crush it with your lips," he said, calling her to task for her obvious lie.

"If you know, why ask?"

"Satisfaction."

"I'm going inside."

"No, I'll let go of you, but stay here just a minute. There are some things that need to be said."

"Evan, I don't—"

"Please."

She stood up, wishing there was a bright light on the patio so she could read his intent on his face.

Standing to be closer to her, he spoke softly but made no move to touch her again.

"A lot has happened in a short time," he began, obviously choosing his words with some thought. "When I insisted you stay, it seemed reasonable to me. You took on a serious responsibility when you brought Gary here. Taking the word of an unscrupulous woman like Sheila was a little foolish. It seemed fair that you see it through."

"Is it through? Have you confirmed that he's your son?"

"No, not yet, and I still think Gary needs you here until it's certain."

"I see."

"No, you don't. I need you too, Dawn, but I'm not going to force you to stay. Here."

He offered her the car keys on the palm of his hand, but she didn't take them. Now that freedom was hers, could she accept it?

"Take them," he insisted, lifting her hand and pressing the keys into it.

"Evan, I don't know what to do."

"I hope you'll stay, but the choice is yours."

"Why have you changed your mind?"

"I suppose it's my way of apologizing," he said, turning his back and walking over to stare out the far screen.

The keys were heavy in her hand, so she tossed them carelessly onto a lounge chair, following him, but not daring to come too close. Was this the end of it, then? She could go and never have to worry about Evan or Gary again. It was what she wanted, of course, but now that she had the means of leaving, a whole web of complications muddled her thoughts. Could she abandon Gary, not knowing who would care for him until his relationship with Evan was confirmed? Her throat tightened at the thought of leaving the little boy she'd come to love, but another pain, sharp and unexpected, hit her with the force of a telling body punch. What she felt for Evan was new and special, unlike anything she had ever experienced before. Giving it a name made it even more impossible to face, but deep inside she knew the truth—she was falling in love with Evan.

Her victory in regaining her keys turned to dust. All that mattered at that moment was the agonizing prospect of never seeing Evan again. Quickly, before he could see how much she was suffering, she turned away and moved to retrieve her keys.

"Dawn!"

His cry seemed like an echo of her own longings, and without thinking, she was in his arms, wrapped in their shelter, deafened by the pounding of his heart and her own as his nearness pushed all thoughts of leaving from her mind.

"Am I forgiven, then?" he asked with an unsuccessful attempt at light bantering.

"There's nothing to forgive. I wanted to stay with you last night, Evan."

"Why did you leave me, then?" he asked, the hurt in his voice unmistakable.

"I was afraid."

"Of me?"

"I don't know. Partly maybe. More afraid of losing part of myself."

"And now?"

His hand moved slowly down her rigid spine, making her shiver with a reaction she didn't want to explore. She didn't respond, because there wasn't any answer.

When his mouth found hers, kissing was too feeble a description of what happened. Her lips, tingling with inexpressible delight, separated to let his tongue flick between them. It tested the slippery biting edge of her teeth, pressing inward to create new sensations. Poised on tiptoe, straining against him, not knowing what course his explorations would take, she trembled in anticipation until he took full possession of her mouth, demanding and taking until her lips ached and her body throbbed with longing.

Just when she thought she'd reached the highest possible peak of human pleasure, his fingers opened the clasp

70

of her bra and began exploring the soft mounds released from their lacy prison.

Like a skater testing a newly frozen pond, she kept edging forward, her delight making her push aside the threat of thin ice ahead. She kept promising herself to stop in just a moment, letting the joy of his touch make her blind to the withdrawal that could soon occur. She passed the point of no return in blissful ignorance of everything but the wild sensations that were rocking her whole being.

Freeing her from the entanglement of her shirt and bra without losing her compliance, Evan grew bolder, bending to caress one hardened peak with his lips.

Her trembling spasm lasted only an instant, but it told him more than a million words could. Scooping her into his arms with the heightened strength born of passion, he carried her to his bed before she could rally her senses enough to protest.

His lips followed wherever his hands went, until he removed the remainder of her clothing with pulse-pounding slowness.

"Evan, we shouldn't," she protested weakly, but he didn't believe her because she wasn't convinced herself. The break in the ice had swallowed her up, but all she felt was a pulsing warmth that wouldn't be denied.

With a clear memory, he leaned over her, still fully dressed himself, unwilling to risk another rejection by rushing to remove his own clothes.

"It's not too late to stop," he whispered, but for Dawn it was. Her body had made the commitment her mind couldn't. Nothing existed at that moment but the passion between them, and she reached for him with hands made unsteady by raw yearning.

Moving slowly, she helped him inch off his clothing, creating undeniable friction wherever she touched him. If a tiny alarm was sounding urgent warnings in the recesses of her brain, she chose not to hear them. Instead of the shock she'd felt before at his nakedness, now she looked at him with tenderness, consumed by an urge to cherish and to please him.

Committed now to what they intended, they tested for love spots, each concerned only with giving sensual joy to the other. Shivers of delight followed his touch as he caressed her back, then let his fingers travel down her spine to gently knead her buttocks. He, in turn, shuddered audibly when her soft hands explored the creases and curvatures of his body.

The enormity of what was happening didn't hit Dawn until the final moment when, for a mad, demoralizing moment, he seemed like a total stranger, and she questioned her own sanity at having gone so far. Then a virtual flood of feelings washed away her last vestige of doubt. Not even the stab of pain, short-lived but excruciating, gave her any regret at that moment.

Floating, she convincingly reassured Evan of her well-being when he anxiously questioned her afterward. She showered him with light, teasing kisses until he cradled her against him with a short burst of laughter, a sound too beautiful to ever forget. Melting together from the heat of their exertions, they settled down to sleep, locked in each other's arms, but only Evan drifted off.

Dawn was too honest with herself to regret what had finally happened, but with physical release had come an unexpected feeling. It hurt to love as much as she loved Evan. She wanted to possess him, own him, keep him by her side forever and ever, and this wish was so alien to anything she'd ever felt for a man before that she didn't know how to cope with it. Because, for a few brief minutes, her life had been so wonderfully complete, she was terrified of the letdown that had to come. Not even in the height of passion had Evan mentioned anything about loving her, and, in truth, nothing had changed between them. Their shared enjoyment didn't bring them any closer to knowing each other better. Thoughts like these robbed Dawn of sleep until pure physical exhaustion finally won out.

Awakening before Evan did with the misty grayness of dawn just penetrating the room, Dawn was mildly surprised to find that she was still the same person. When his first move of the day was to seek and to find her lips, she knew she was wrong. She did feel different.

"Good morning," he mumbled, rubbing his nose against hers.

Cradling her head on his chest, he lazily played with one dark ringlet of her hair, wrapping it around his finger. She snuggled closer, loving the softness of his chest hair under her cheek and the slightly salty tang of his skin when she flicked it with her tongue. In the clarity of the new day she momentarily managed to put aside all the doubts that had plagued her sleepless hours.

He groaned, then said, "I have to get up."

"It's not even daylight."

She wrapped her arms around him as though she could hold him there with physical force.

"It will be soon. I have to take a shower."

"I'll take one with you."

"Give me a raincheck."

"A raincheck for the shower?"

"It's important, sweetheart. I have to see a man from the university about an experimental crop in one of my fields, and an early breakfast meeting was all he could manage before he leaves for Africa for two months."

He disentangled himself, but not without telling her how reluctant he was to leave her. What started as a friendly kiss on her forehead became a whole series of slow, shivery ones, until Dawn was sure he wouldn't really go right away. She underestimated his self-control; Evan wasn't a man to be ruled by his wants alone.

"Witch!" he teased, giving her a playful slap on her rear. "Go back to sleep and let a man make a living."

With her mind so filled with Evan, she was anything but sleepy. She needed something from him, but she didn't know how to talk to him about it. For the first time in her life she had given herself totally to a man, and she didn't know how she felt about it.

When he came back into the room, his hair damp and only a towel wrapped around him, her feelings of uneasiness only grew.

He threw aside the towel and began dressing without a trace of self-consciousness, as though they'd shared a room for ages. Studying the length of his body, Dawn tried to analyze why the varied shades of his skin were so exciting, when they would be amusing on anyone else. His face and neck were deeply tanned with an undertone of redness from recent exposure to the fierce rays of the summer sun, and his back was a golden bronze from running a tractor without a shirt earlier in the season. His legs were only lightly tinted, and where the sun never reached, his flesh was fair and softer-looking, as though part of him were vulnerable in spite of his aggressive masculinity.

She wanted him to come to her then, but it was a purely physical feeling, overcome by a growing reserve. What had happened between them hadn't broken down any real barriers. It had only piled complication on top of complication and given her what seemed to be a hopeless heartache. She didn't want to love Evan; she didn't want to desire him as a lover. But she did just that.

"I'll make a deal with you," he said, swooping down on her for a very quick kiss. "You duck back under the covers and don't slow me down, and I'll come home for lunch. What time does Gary take his nap?"

"Around one o'clock usually," she said.

After he cheerfully told her good-bye, she didn't try to

hold back the hot tears that were filling her eyes. In the past she had always been the one who set the restrictions and ended the relationships she'd had with men. Her dating had been a casual thing, and her affection was given and withdrawn with little discomfort to herself. She'd never even suspected that love could cause such pain—the searing, soul-searching agony that was nothing like her girlish images of romance.

"Oh, damn," she said aloud, burying her wet face in the pillow that still held just a trace of Evan's enticing scent. The last thing she'd wanted was to fall in love, and the worst person she could have chosen was Evan. He was rooted to his land, encumbered with the complications of an unsuccessful former marriage, and he'd probably only taken advantage of a convenient opportunity for sex. Even if he did care about her as a person, what could come of it? She had been unfair to let him think that anything had changed. She still had a great job opportunity and a fresh new future waiting for her in California, and she would be a fool to lose sight of that.

Even dozing off again didn't make the morning seem short. She found lots to do alone in the house with Gary, but her mind was never far from Evan. Life had a different hue because she was living in anticipation of his return, but her feelings were so confused that she could hardly concentrate. At least nothing Gary did could irritate her, not even when he knocked over a plant, forcing her to carefully remove all the spilled dirt from the carpet. Knowing that Evan would be back in only a few hours gave her unexpected reserves of patience. Gary's antics were trifles easily handled compared to her anxiety, and her dread about facing Evan in a normal daytime situation.

Always happiest when she was busy, she couldn't work hard enough to exhaust her surplus energy. The end of the morning found her outside playing hide-and-seek with

Gary under the giant, low-hanging limbs of a spruce. A brisk wind made the heat a little more tolerable, but she was glad when it was finally time for lunch.

Evan didn't join them for lunch, but Dawn wasn't disappointed about that. The promise in his voice that morning suggested that he wasn't coming home for food anyway, but she didn't feel at all ready to consider a repeat of the previous night. Even though she thought of little else, and remembering made her ache with longing, she just couldn't step into a casual affair with Evan. She had never surrendered to her own sensuality before, and having done so with him was making her reexamine herself with painful thoroughness. What did she expect from life? Could this strange emotional surge she felt with Evan be powerful enough to turn her well-ordered life upside down? Maybe in the light of mundane, everyday concerns, she would discover it was temporary madness. Whatever the eventual outcome, she needed time to patch together her own personality and evaluate her attraction to Evan. It was the way she had always done things—clearheadedly, logically. At least she could salvage that much from their encounter.

Gary toyed with his vegetable soup and smeared peanut butter everywhere, even in his hair, so Dawn lugged him away and popped him into the tub rather than trying to clean him up piecemeal. Bath time was fun time for the child, so he didn't mind the extra dunking a bit; in fact, he tried to stall as long as possible, much preferring a good splash in the tub to a nap.

Evan found them in the bathroom, Gary still in the bathtub, with Dawn on her knees, trying to drain the water and collect his toys. As usual Gary was squirming, a natural state for him.

"I'll get him," Evan offered, lifting the slippery little body from the tub and wrapping him in a big orange towel. "Go and get your britches on, Gary, and I'll tuck you in for your nap."

Running from the bathroom with Indian whoops, Gary didn't see Evan take Dawn in his arms. He missed the mutual moan of pleasure and the look when their eyes met.

Whatever Evan said to Gary, it worked. Moments later there was nothing but silence to be heard in his room.

"Can I fix you some lunch?"

"Yes, but I'll start with dessert," he said, pulling her into his arms and kissing her in a way that made her forget for a brief instant all her doubts of the morning.

"Evan, your lunch," Dawn said, pulling away but not without reluctance.

Keeping his hands on her arms, he looked at her so intently that she had to drop her eyes.

"About last night," he said softly.

"Not now," she said, panic rising in spite of her best efforts to stay calm.

"I should have known," he said, obviously not sure how to phrase what he wanted to say, "that it was your first time."

"It doesn't matter," she said, her attempt at casualness sounding off-hand and flip instead.

He frowned and released her, torn between disbelief and irritation.

"I think it does."

"Look, can I fix you a roast beef sandwich?"

He looked exasperated, but decided to play it her way. "Sure, I'd appreciate it."

CHAPTER FIVE

"I told the Clatts we'd have dinner with them this evening," Evan said, walking to the patio with Dawn after
lunch, letting one arm fall lightly around her waist.

"You told them, did you?" Dawn asked. The heat wave
was still raging, and she felt a light film of moisture above
her lip as soon as they left the comfort of the air-conditioning.

"They invited us, so I gave them an answer. You don't
mind, do you?" he asked, sounding somewhat surprised at
her tone.

He studied her face, tempted by the slightly flushed look
that reminded him vividly of their lovemaking.

"No, of course not," she answered quickly, but the
truth was that she didn't feel like going and she wasn't
sure why.

Was dinner with the neighbors just a little too cozy, too
domestic? Or did she feel uneasy because Evan had accepted for her without any thought of consulting her first? The
two of them needed to talk; they needed it very badly. He
seemed to have lost sight of the fact that she was on her
way to California. Sometimes she felt the same way, and
that alarmed her even more.

"Have you heard anything from your lawyer lately?"
she asked, feeling in a mildly combative mood. This was
an important subject that they'd been ignoring lately.

"Yes, but it's all negative. If Gary was born in Chicago,

then his record must be lost or recorded under a false name, not Peg's maiden name or mine. Cliff has a detective working on it, one he's used before with good results. But so far the birth certificate hasn't been found."

"Evan, that's terrible."

"Not all terrible," he said, so close to her now that she could hardly remember what they were talking about.

He kissed her then, pulling her head to his and savoring her lips without making any demands. It was a deep, affectionate kiss, the one kind that she could accept without feeling pressured or threatened.

"Gary's invited too," he said, forcing himself to move away from her, but standing and admiring her for a long moment.

That evening as he waited for Evan on the patio, Gary was wild with excitement, but Dawn was more than a little depressed. Rushing in at the last minute, Evan needed to shower and change before the dinner, but she wished he'd decide to cancel. Her reluctance to go to the Clatts made her feel snobbish, but it wasn't that at all. She just didn't want to be engulfed by the warmth of their family circle. She didn't want to hear about Tammy's new boyfriend or Peter's prize-winning 4-H hog. Being with them, sharing their interests, and hearing about their everyday concerns made her care about them, and she had too many ties to sever already. She felt more and more as if her life were racing out of control, and deadlines were catching up with her.

A second phone call to Maggie the day before made her departure more urgent. Her friend's supervisor had received Dawn's résumé and was definitely interested, but he was already starting to interview for the opening in Maggie's department. He couldn't delay his decision very long, so it was imperative that Dawn reach Los Angeles soon.

Watching Evan walk from the barn to the house had etched a whole new set of impressions of him on Dawn's mind, and she pondered them as she waited. Though he'd moved with a grace that not even his fatigue could disguise, he worked too hard; it was as though he'd dedicated his whole life to this struggle with the land. He had too many acres and too many problems, and she desperately wanted there to be more in life for him than worry and hard labor. She wasn't sure just what that should be, but his need for someone to love was evident. He tried to hide the scars of his first marriage, but they were there nevertheless. If proof that Gary was his son could be found, Evan would never need to feel that his life was empty again. It would make their parting so much easier too, at least for him.

"Give me ten more minutes," he said, smiling at both of them as he popped his head through the doorway for an instant. "I need to shave, but Dewey was running behind schedule too. I'm sure his wife is used to it."

"I know, the trials and tribulations of a farmer's wife," Dawn said wryly, then regretted it immediately. Marriage was one thing Evan hadn't mentioned, and she didn't want him to think she was bringing it up.

Betty Clatt's dinner was marvelous; no other word could be used to describe it. She barbecued pork on the outside grill, and her sweet corn, cooked the same way and dripping with butter, had to be the best in the world. Serving homemade blueberry pie for dessert was like silver plating a bar of gold; nothing could top the main course.

Gary got lots of attention from the Clatts' children, who were old enough to be amused by his antics, and the men settled down to talk corn, land, and politics, the three staples of conversation in Iowa. That Evan was well informed didn't exactly surprise Dawn, but she still marveled at the fact that farmers were so politically astute and so vocal about their views. It was nothing like the indifference of most of the people she'd always known, perhaps because the fate of every new crop depended so heavily on what the federal government was doing.

She enjoyed Betty's after-dinner chatter as they cleaned up together, but her uneasiness tempered her pleasure. Dawn's viewpoint seemed to be out of focus, like a photograph taken by a moving camera, and she didn't feel sure about anything anymore. California seemed remote and a little threatening, instead of alive with promise as it had been only a short time ago. But because she was so unsure of her future, she was all the more impatient to get on with it. Parting with Evan and Gary was going to hurt, and she couldn't stand the dread she felt much longer. Like major surgery, it was better to face up to it and get it done. Betty's obvious contentment with her own life made Dawn feel at a disadvantage in talking with her, having to grope for common ground even though she liked Betty very much.

"It's so good to see Evan happy again," Betty said, completely switching away from the topic they'd been discussing. "His divorce really threw him. He's the forever type, you know."

Did she believe that? Dawn wondered, but replied with a vague "Oh."

"He's been so great to us," Betty went on without any urging. "When Dewey lost his job at the meat-packing plant that closed a few years ago, I don't know what we would have done if Evan hadn't persuaded him to give farming another try."

"Oh, dear, there goes Gary!" Dawn cried, seeing the three-year-old take a tumble as he ran across the yard.

"Oh, he's not hurt," Betty said, peering out the window, but Dawn insisted on running out to check, welcoming any excuse to break off their conversation. She'd heard enough about Evan for one evening.

* * *

When they returned home, they tumbled Gary into bed together, sharing his last sleepy moments of the day as if they were a pair of doting parents. When Gary called Dawn back for one more good-night hug, Dawn went, even though she knew it was one of his many delaying tactics. His little arms around her neck made her heart swell with love, but the extra moment alone with him didn't give her enough time to decide how to face Evan.

If she'd entertained a wild hope of escaping directly to her room, Evan frustrated it. When she closed Gary's door, he was there in the hallway, waiting for her.

"You can't avoid talking to me forever," he said gently, taking her arm and steering her toward the neutral territory of the family room.

"Would you like me to make some coffee?" she asked.

"You can't put me off with food or drink."

He drew her down beside him on the couch, but, mercifully, he didn't try to touch her.

"Look," he said, trying to be patient and understanding, "I'm not so old I can't remember what it's like the first time, so I think we should talk."

"There's nothing to say," she said, feeling totally inadequate for any serious discussion.

"You're shutting me out, Dawn," he said. "I don't like the feeling."

"I'm sorry," she said woodenly, still refusing to meet his gaze.

"No, that won't do. Are you angry? Hurt? Sorry? I have to know why you're doing this about-face."

"I don't know why."

Her voice was a plea, but he chose to ignore it.

"Last night, Dawn, you wanted to be with me. It wasn't like the other night. I'd swear to that."

"Evan, just drop it for now," she said desperately, getting up to move away from him. "You act as if I've accused you of a crime."

"I told you I don't like games," he said, fighting back his anger with visible effort. "Will you come to bed with me now, Dawn?"

There was challenge, not passion, in his voice, and she reacted angrily.

"Isn't it convenient, having a temporary live-in bed partner?" she lashed out.

"What is wrong with you? You wanted to make love last night. Don't pretend you didn't enjoy it!"

"I'm not pretending anything!"

"I'm waiting for an answer."

When she didn't answer, he pulled her into his arms, kissing her forcefully with more anger than passion. She rubbed her abused lips with the back of her hand when he released her, spitting out an answer under the spur of his hostile aggression.

"You can go to bed alone!"

"I see," he said curtly, and left the room.

You don't see at all, she thought miserably, hurrying to her room as soon as she heard his door bang shut behind him. How easy it would have been to go with him, to be fired by his touch and engulfed by his lovemaking. Even after his angry reaction, she had to steel herself not to go to his door and beg to come in. She felt limp with longing and exhausted by her emotional struggle.

Hours later, lying sleepless, she made her decision; she would leave the next day. Tears escaped from her tightly closed eyelids, but she was sure this was what she should do. Proof of Gary's birth might be lost forever, and if she was ever going, it had to be soon; further delay would only make it more painful. As it was, her experiences with Evan had changed her in ways she had yet to understand. The longer she stayed near him, the greater the risk to all her carefully made plans for her future. Her life would be so simple if only she could erase all traces of the love she felt for Evan.

Staying in bed, she let Evan leave the house in the morning without talking to him. Her strongest instinct told her to leave while he was gone and spare them both a parting scene, but for several reasons she decided not to take the coward's way out. First, of course, she couldn't leave Gary alone, and she didn't know whom to call to baby-sit.

She couldn't ask Tammy without alerting the whole Clatt family, and Evan worked too closely with them. Also, Evan seemed to have reclaimed her keys; when she went to look for them on the patio the day after he'd returned them, they weren't there. She'd shook out all the cushions, regretting over and over that she hadn't followed her father's advice about a spare set. When she purchased her used car, the former owner had already lost the spares, and Dawn hadn't bothered to duplicate the remaining set. Until she came to Iowa, she'd never lost anything, let alone something as important as her car keys. Or her heart, she added to herself.

These were the practical reasons, but even if they could be overlooked, she wouldn't leave Evan without saying good-bye. As vague and undefined as their relationship was, it was too important to sever it without letting him know. Loving him as she did, she had to try to eradicate the bitterness between them.

Her plans were simple enough. Somehow, between watching Gary and telling Evan, she would pack her things, then drive to Des Moines, find a motel, and spend the rest of the day crying her heart out. When that was over, she'd get on with her life and try to pretend that she'd bypassed Iowa on her way west. It didn't sound like a very good plan, unlikely as it was that she'd ever stop loving Evan, but it was the best she could devise.

Getting her bags laid out on the bed wasn't tough, but reorganizing them to hold the portion of her clothes she'd unpacked was a beastly job. Gary did everything imaginable to slow her down, rightly sensing that what she was doing wasn't to his advantage and getting into trouble faster than she could work. He deserved to be sent to his room, but she did want to spend as much time with him as possible before she left. A lump in her throat prevented her from eating, but she fed Gary lunch and put him down for his nap. By then it was too late to finish packing before Evan came back to the house. She had hoped to be ready to leave, but the job of gathering her possessions was easy compared to facing him.

After priming herself all morning to tell him, bracing herself for his reaction, whatever it would be, she never had the opportunity.

He'd picked up the mail from the box by the road and was reading a letter at the kitchen table when she found him. His profanity as he read startled her; he rarely needed strong language to express exactly what he wanted to say. But not even his language prepared her for the savage anger he directed at her the instant he saw her.

"Here's the bottom line at last," he said furiously, "as if you weren't expecting it."

"What are you talking about?"

"Your friend Sheila. Did she tell you how much she was going to ask, or didn't you stick around for all the details?"

"Will you please tell me what's the matter?"

"Cute, Dawn, cute. Pretend you aren't in on this."

He stood up, tossing the letter on the table with an expression that dared her to read it.

It didn't take long to read; Sheila's demands were simple. Unless Evan reimbursed her for three years expense and trouble, she'd come to reclaim Gary.

"She can't do this," Dawn said, too stunned to react to the insinuations Evan had made.

"No? You're smarter than that, Dawn. You know she can and probably will. I don't have a shred of proof that

85

Gary is mine, or have you forgotten that detail the same way you've forgotten quite a few other things? Your integrity, for one thing."

"You can't accuse me of any part in this!"

"I can't? Who brought Gary here without any proof of his birth? Who insisted that I be kind, take an interest, become attached?"

"Only for his sake!"

"So I'd be willing to bribe Sheila to keep him!"

"No!"

"Was sleeping with me part of the plan, so you could stay here and bring the two of us together?"

Overwhelmed by feelings stronger than simple anger, she could only accuse him in return. "That was your idea!"

"I was easy. I'll admit that. You made me realize that celibacy isn't much fun. Sheila must have guessed I'd be a pushover."

"I never intended to stay here. You made me."

"I told you that you could go before we—"

"Then took my keys back the next day," she interrupted, unable to bear hearing any reference to their lovemaking.

"I didn't take your damn keys again."

"I looked. They weren't on the patio in the morning."

"Then why wait until now to mention it?"

"It's impossible to talk sensibly to you."

"You're some person to talk about not communicating. I did everything but get down on my knees and beg to know what was wrong with you. Now I know. Playing Mata Hari is a little tougher than you thought. I was a damn fool to believe your act about being a naive little social worker. I'm so stupid, I worried about hurting you."

"It wasn't an act, and I don't know anything about Sheila, but you go ahead and believe whatever you like."

86

Their furious exchange was carried on in harsh, muted voices, the medium of angry adults who don't want to be heard by a child, but greater volume couldn't have conveyed the depth of their anger any more forcefully. Dawn ran from the room, blinded by tears of sheer rage, not the sad droplets she'd expected after their parting.

She ran to her room, but she wasn't able to lock her door before Evan reached it. When he saw the suitcases open on the bed, it was the face of an enraged stranger that loomed over her.

"You were packing." The flat dull tone of his voice only hinted at the fury that was boiling inside.

"I was going to tell you. I have to go to California now, or I'll lose any chance at the job I want. You knew when I came that I was going there. I never said otherwise."

"Why didn't you tell me yesterday you were leaving when I wanted to make love to you, or the night before when you nearly drove me crazy I wanted you so badly?"

"Stop it!" she screamed.

"Oh, does it bother you to hear a recap of your amorous adventure, now that your job here is done?"

"My only job was to bring Gary to his father. It was a terrible mistake. I wish I'd never seen you!"

"At least be honest with me. How much did Sheila tell you? Did she promise you a share of the money if you pulled this off?"

"You have no right to talk like that!"

"If you talk about rights to me again, you'll regret it." His whole body was tense and threatening.

"I do already! What will you do, beat me? My God, I was going to leave Gary here alone with you."

"Now you remember Gary! Don't you think you're a little late? Were you going to take him with you? No, of course not! If you did, it would spoil the plan. You were going to be packed and ready for your retreat when the letter came."

"Sheila's letter has nothing to do with my leaving!"

"No? You just happened to be packing when it arrived?"

With both hands he sent the closest suitcase flying across the room, then totally cleared the bed of her possessions by yanking the spread from under them. If the floor had opened up and swallowed him, she wouldn't have been more dumbfounded. The calm, controlled man was gone, and the impossible had happened; she was afraid of Evan.

"Dawn, I'm not sleepy."

For an awful moment Dawn was terrified that Evan would turn his anger on the child standing in the doorway, but he shook off his rage with an almost visible shudder and walked over to the boy. Sweeping him up, Evan carried him back to his room, and Dawn could hear his firm but not unkind orders to Gary.

"You stay in bed until you're told to come out," Evan said. "If you're not sleepy, you can look at your books."

To actually feel her own legs and arms trembling was such a novel sensation that it partially distracted Dawn from the emotional upheaval between them, then Evan was filling the doorway with his presence, every fiber in his body straining from his anger.

"Why were you packing?"

He shut the door behind him and locked it.

"I have to leave. It has nothing to do with Gary or Sheila . . . or you."

"When were you going to leave? Before or after we went to bed again?"

"What kind of a question is that? We aren't going to bed again!"

"A direct one, and I want an answer." He moved several steps closer and his height wasn't perfect for her anymore; he seemed overpoweringly large. "Were you going to tell me at all?"

"I—I planned to talk when you came home this after-noon."

"Just talk?"

"Yes."

"About what?"

"About why I have to leave. I need a job, Evan. I'll lose my chance if I don't leave. Maggie can't hold the apartment for me indefinitely. I never dreamed I'd be here this long—"

"It's been days, not years," he interrupted.

Wonderful days, she thought, *but they have to end.*

"Because Sheila finally made her move?"

"No!"

"For God's sake, Dawn, at least be truthful with me!"

"Because your wife lied to you? Is that why, Evan? Am I supposed to pay her debt to you?"

"My ex-wife has nothing to do with this."

"I think she does. You don't trust me because you didn't trust her, but I'm a different person, Evan."

The look in his eyes was worse than anything that had come before. She turned away, unable to stand the cold disdain that was more terrible than raw hatred.

"Save your Psychology One-oh-one theories for your welfare clients," he said cruelly; then he left her alone.

She didn't even see the chaos in the room where her possessions lay scattered everywhere; the turbulence in her mind blinded her to everything but her pain. Always an easy crier, she didn't shed a tear, but the hurt was all the deeper because of it. She felt stunned, imbedded in a hard, unyielding shell like the Eskimo forever imprisoned in glass on the bedroom shelf. If she moved, her brittle bones would shatter to dust.

When the initial shock wore off, Dawn felt a burning rage unlike anything she'd ever experienced. Sheila again! And Evan believed that she was capable of helping that unprincipled bitch. Without the concern of friendly neighbors in the building, Gary would have been deprived of almost everything a child has a right to expect—love, care, stimulation, training, toys, and excursions. Dawn wasn't the only neighbor who'd watched him carefully for signs of abuse. If Gary hadn't had the attention of unusually kind people, who knows what would have happened? Now Sheila had the nerve to demand money from Evan for her indifferent care. How could Evan think she was helping Sheila? She hated herself for loving him and for the suffering her feelings for him had caused her.

She wanted to throw things, to kick and scream, to lash out at his awful accusation, but, lacking a target, she began furiously trying to right the mess he'd made of her packing. Working like a person possessed, she finally undid the damage he'd done and managed to stuff everything into one piece of luggage or another. It would take her weeks to repair and reorganize everything, but nothing mattered now. It was clear that she had to leave immediately.

But what should she do about Gary?

She couldn't take him, and she couldn't leave him. If Gary was Evan's child, it wouldn't be beyond him to accuse her of kidnaping; if he wasn't, how would she explain his presence in California? Would Maggie want a three-year-old roommate? Who would care for him while she worked? Would Sheila trace them and reclaim the boy? The hopelessness of the muddle brought tears to her eyes at last, and she sat on the edge of the bed, letting them run unchecked down her face.

"Dawn!"

Gary's impatient call told her very plainly that this wasn't his day to sleep. She dashed cold water on her face, for all the good it did, then went in to release him from his confinement.

If Evan was telling the truth about her keys, there were two possibilities. Either Mrs. Winsch had found them and put them someplace, or Gary'd appropriated them as a plaything.

"Gary, remember my keys, the keys that make the car go? Do you have them, honey?"

She got smirks and giggles, but no help, although he hugely enjoyed the game of hunt-the-keys. It took most of the long, unhappy afternoon, but she finally found them wedged between two logs in the wood box by the fireplace. There was no doubt about how they got there.

Now that she had the means to go, she had to think about Gary. Again she ran up against the same impossible obstacles: she couldn't leave him, and she couldn't take him. She couldn't stay with Evan, and she hated even the thought of leaving the only man who'd ever awakened a woman's love in her. Her head was pounding from an agonizing headache, and all she wanted to do was pass out and wake up with all her problems solved.

Going from the comfort of the house into the scorched air outside magnified the pain in her head, but playing outside with Gary did distract her. The heat didn't seem to faze him, and they stayed out until it was time for him to go to bed.

Evan hadn't returned for dinner, and as soon as Gary was settled for the night, Dawn went to her room. Knowing that she was hiding from her problems and from him, she locked the door to the hallway and lay on the bed fully dressed. The smoothness of the pillow eased her headache slightly, but she was much too agitated to sleep. The confrontation with Evan kept playing through her mind like a bad movie, more upsetting with each run-through. What could she have said or done differently? Nothing, absolutely nothing. Once she took it upon herself to bring Gary to his father, everything fell into place with a fatalistic inevitability.

She shouldn't have trusted Sheila, and she shouldn't have fallen in love with Evan.

Suddenly the whole story ran amuck in her mind, and she sat upright, pressing her temples with rigid hands. Admitting it made everything that much worse. She was in love with Evan, a painful, ill-advised love that was the last thing she needed or wanted. The physical attraction was only a part of it, and no amount of quarreling or misunderstanding could take the edge off her feelings. After what had happened today, things could never be completely right between them. How could she live in the shadow of a man whose first marriage had left him bitter and distrustful? Relationships only started in bed, and hers with Evan had no place to go from there. At this moment she hated him as passionately as she loved him. Why had he insisted she stay? If he'd accepted his very likely relationship to Gary, she would be in California now, happily employed in a challenging new job. Damn him, anyway!

The knock on her door was soft, not demanding, and for a moment she thought Gary might have wandered out of bed. Her pause in answering was well considered; Evan said her name several times, then turned the handle. When he found it locked, there was no more sound on the other side of the door.

Dawn buried her head in the pillow, using all her strength of will to keep from answering him. There was nothing to be said between them right now. When she felt calmer, more dispassionate, she'd arrange a time to leave, making sure he had someone to care for Gary while he worked. Feeling as if she'd just made a sensible, workable decision, however painful it was, she relaxed a little and closed her eyes. Her headache had subsided somewhat, helped as much by a returning measure of calmness as by the double dose of aspirin she'd swallowed.

"Dawn."

His voice was so close, she sat upright with a start.

"I didn't mean to startle you," he said softly. "The bathroom door wasn't locked."

"Anyone else would have respected one locked door," she said, using indignation to mask a host of more turbulent feelings.

"It's hard to talk through a door."

He sat on the edge of the bed, his hands resting just inches from where she sat rigidly upright. Sensing her disadvantage, she moved hurriedly to the far side and put her feet on the floor, keeping her face hidden from him.

"I have a headache, Evan. I'd rather be alone."

"Listen for just a minute. Then if you want me to leave, I will."

"There's nothing more to say."

"There's a lot."

He walked to her side of the bed and sat down beside her, fortunately making no move to touch her. One gesture from him might release the floodgate, and she didn't want to give him the satisfaction of seeing her cry.

"Please go," she begged.

"Not until you hear me out. I'll start by saying I'm sorry."

She shook her head; this wasn't what she wanted to hear. Anger, fighting, yelling—these were things she could handle. It wasn't fair to use tenderness as a weapon.

"Dawn, I was upset, and I took it out on you. I don't really believe you'd be a part of Sheila's scheme. She used you, and she's trying to use me. I bottled up a lot of resentment when Peg left me, and you just happened to be in the way when the explosion finally came."

He was saying all the right things. Why did it hurt so much?

"Dawn, look at me!"

He cupped her face in his hands, his misery plainly etched on his. Her eyes, when they met his, were filmy with tears, and he leaned forward to catch one errant drop with his lips.

The only escape from his scrutiny was to press her face against his chest, and she did so just as the whole day's accumulation of tears burst loose. Sobbing beyond control, she soaked his shirt front and didn't refuse the handkerchief he pressed on her. The soft caress of his hand on her hair and the warmth of his breath on her forehead didn't help at all.

"My friends always called me a crybaby," she said, at last mopping what she hoped were the last of her tears with his soggy hanky.

"Your friends were right," he said, but there was tenderness, not mockery, in his voice.

He kissed her face, damp and red as she knew it must be, trailing his lips from her swollen lids to the softness of her parted lips.

"My favorite flavor," he said lightly. "Salty strawberry."

"There's no such thing," she managed to say without too much sobbing.

"Dawn."

She didn't know it was possible to be held so tightly without being hurt.

"I'm a mess," she said.

"A beautiful mess."

"Evan, let me wash my face."

He released her, and she escaped to dash handful after handful of chilly water over her face. She knew that when she went back to her room, Evan would make love to her. Even with the door closed she could see him in her imagination, removing his clothes, stretching out on her bed, waiting for her to come to him, as though the contact of their bodies could erase everything else. Part of her rebelled at the tyranny of his physical attraction, but anoth-

94

er part, deeper, hidden, defying analysis, knew that she wanted to make love as much as he did.

She took her time, but there was no call from her room, no impatient sounds, no knock to urge her to hurry. Slowly and deliberately she removed all her clothes, leaving them in a careless pile on top of her sandals. Addicted as she was to warm, caressing showers, she turned the cold water on full force and stepped under its punishing spray, taking the full impact of the icy jets on her shoulders and backside. It took real courage to turn her sensitive breasts into the onslaught, but she endured the pain with spartan impassiveness.

When she emerged, she was shaking horribly, but her head felt better. Evan's terry robe was hanging on the back of the door, and, wrapping it around her, she felt as if she'd arrived home after being lost in a blizzard. Some of his warmth seemed to cling to the robe, and she hugged her arms across her chest, trying to draw strength from his garment like an ancient priestess practicing sympathetic magic.

Being decisive took far more courage than stepping under an icy shower, but as her body warmed, her resolve hardened. Devastating as Evan's accusations had been, she could forgive him for thinking she had helped Sheila. Bringing Gary without contacting Evan first had been a serious mistake, one she was paying for dearly. She believed that Sheila's letter had only released a host of buried hurts and frustrations, and she had received more than her due of his anger because Peg and Sheila were beyond his reach.

Forgiving someone you love isn't all that difficult, leaving him would be. If she went to his arms now, Dawn was sure she would lose control of her own life. She would become a hanger-on in his life, waiting to see whether he'd make a commitment to her, gorging herself on physical love without knowing whether his feelings went deeper.

She stared at the door dejectedly, hating what she had to do but unable to see any other course. If Evan was still there, and she never doubted it, she had to reject him in a way that would free her to leave in the morning. She had to do it, but it was going to hurt terribly.

As she expected, Evan was stretched out on the bed, but not in the way she'd imagined. Not only was he fully dressed, he was sound asleep.

"Oh, Evan," she whispered aloud, more touched by his weariness than she would have been by any declaration of love, display of passion, or argument against her decision.

Carefully, trying hard not to wiggle the bed, she crept beside him, wrapping the folds of his oversize robe around her legs. His hand was lying limply by his side, and she let herself touch it with a feathery caress, so light that he didn't react to it in his sleep. If she woke him, she would have to give him her carefully planned speech telling him that their relationship had begun and ended in one impossibly wonderful evening. Lying beside him, she felt too emotionally drained to handle it; the morning was soon enough. She would be able to face the final break a hundred times better after some much-needed rest.

She thought she was too conscious of his even breathing, his relaxed body, his latent sexuality, to possibly sleep, but she was wrong. In moments a deep, healing sleep claimed her too.

Dawn was the time of day that gave her a name, but she'd never really appreciated it before. As the room gradually became lighter, she thought of the relief ancient peoples must have felt each morning when they saw proof that the sun hadn't failed them and doomed them to eternal darkness. Realizing that Evan was still beside her gave her just a glimmer of a similar relief, but her decision came back to her. These might be her last truly happy moments for some time, so she didn't wake him to tell him she was leaving him.

His hand was heavy on the side of her breast, and she moved slightly, but he didn't remove it. Instead he tucked it more securely in a pleasurable spot, her movement making his fingers come alive, caressing her with full awareness of what he was doing.

He was playing a game with her, pretending sleep while arousing her to full wakefulness, his leg shifting to entrap hers.

"I know you're awake," she said accusingly.

"How?" he mumbled sleepily.

"You're nice when you're asleep."

"Isn't this nice?" He pulled her vigorously into his grasp, kissing her soundly on the end of her nose.

"Well. . . ."

"You'll regret that, woman."

She thought of telling him then, but his teasing mood put her off.

His next kiss shook her to her toes, and she didn't need further prompting to shift the length of her body closer to his, reaching out to caress his now familiar warmth with eager hands.

"What are you wearing?" he asked, disentangling her from the belt around her waist.

"Your robe. I took a cold shower. Who are you to talk about bedroom attire?"

"Oh, Lord, did I sleep all night in these clothes?"

"Unless you're a sleepwalker, you did."

"Honey, I'm sorry."

"Don't be. I like you when you're musky and soiled and worn out."

"When I'm vulnerable like one of your case histories, you mean."

"Evan!"

"I'm not starting a fight," he said passionately. "I want you too badly. Do you want me to take a shower?"

"No, no, I don't," she said, capturing his hand and

hugging it against her, loving the hardness of his palm, the swell of calluses, the downy hair on the back of it that was bleached almost colorless by an unrelenting Iowa sun.

Now was the time to tell him, but her resolve weakened as he slipped his hand under the robe, arousing her with firm caresses that clouded her mind as they fired her passion.

It was as though all their rest through the night had been a gathering of energies to be unleashed in the pursuit of mutual pleasure. His gentle, coaxing manners were forgotten, and he demanded and took what he wanted. Far from resenting it, she responded with growing intensity, released at least temporarily from all her restraining doubts.

Afterward they lay entwined in a trancelike doze, unwilling to signal an end to their lovemaking, unable to recreate the peak. Her mind was empty of everything but the aftermath of physical sensations, and Dawn couldn't will herself to face her own decisions, not now. Being next to him filled her whole being with peace.

Evan hated sleeping with cold, stale air, so the windows were always opened at night, the whir of the air-conditioner silenced. The air that stole through the open window was unbelievably hot for so early in the morning, making them doubly sluggish.

"It's morning, I'm afraid," he said softly, cradling her head more firmly against his shoulder.

"A farmer's work is never done?" she teased, wanting desperately to prolong this moment of utter happiness.

"Never."

"I found my keys," she blurted out impulsively.

"Oh?"

"Gary hid them in the wood box."

"Smart boy. Wish I'd thought of it."

"Maybe you did."

"Not my style."

"No, it wouldn't be, would it?" she mused.

"Are you going to use them?" His voice had an undertone of dead seriousness now.

"I don't know, Evan." After being so sure of herself the night before, she was dismayed by her answer.

Reading the pain in her indecisiveness, he lay absolutely motionless; even his breath seemingly suspended.

"What can I say?"

"Would you try to stop me?"

"Yes."

"By taking my keys?"

"No, not by force. I promise you that."

"How, then?"

"This way."

He gathered her into his arms, persuasiveness in every atom of his body, possessing her with a gentle ease that was as deceptive as the beginning of a brush fire.

The work day was going to be a short one; even experienced field hands in protective hats would be foolish to strain under the dehydrating rays of the noonday sun. Dewey looked at his watch for the third time in as many minutes, debating whether to call Evan's house. It was the first time he'd ever known Evan to be late to work.

CHAPTER SIX

What was it about a man that could hold a woman in mental bondage? Dawn wondered as she watched Gary pushing his truck through every possible obstacle course that the patio furniture suggested to him. Once, working in the Welfare Department, she'd had a battered young woman come to her to apply for aid. When Dawn saw the vivid mass of purple bruises on one side of her face and arm, she was ready to call the police, legal aid, or even the fire department if necessary, to save the woman from further beatings.

"Sister, you just mind your own business," the woman had told her in considerably saltier language.

Appalled at the woman's unwillingness to protect herself, Dawn had used every conceivable argument to try to get her to leave the man who wasn't even her husband, or at least get some professional help. In the end, the woman caused quite a fuss and involved Dawn's supervisor. The battered woman insisted that she'd come for money, not advice, and nobody was going to tell her how to run her life. At last Dawn was forced to process her application without referring her to anyone else for help with her abusive lover.

"Why do you stay with him?" Dawn dared to ask when the woman's good humor was restored by the prospect of financial aid.

"If you ever had a man you really loved, you wouldn't hafta ask."

The incident had bothered Dawn for a long time, sure as she was that the woman was making a tragic mistake, one that could endanger her health and possibly even her life. Not even her supervisor's philosophical advice that "you can't help people who don't want to be helped" was any comfort.

Thinking about the incident as she watched Gary play, Dawn saw something in herself that she didn't like. She had felt so superior because that kind of situation couldn't happen to her; she would never let her feelings for any man overrule her own good common sense, or so she had thought. What priggishness that battered woman must have seen in her, as if her theories were more potent than the chemistry between a man and a woman who loved each other and wanted to be together. In retrospect Dawn realized that she might have helped the woman if she'd shown more compassion and understanding. When one man becomes the whole focus of a woman's life, no amount of well-intentioned advice could alter her feelings, but more sympathy might have persuaded her to get counseling for both of them. *Meddling!* That was Evan's word for what she did!

Gary was playing contentedly, but Dawn was too restless to sit placidly watching him. When she was with Evan, there was noplace else she wanted to be, but when he was away, which was often, she felt like one of those jointed wooden dolls that dances on a string. A skillful handler could make one of the folksy dolls perform on a board like a creature possessed, just the way Evan could beckon to her and transform her into a woman possessed by passion.

Her other self—cool, calm, and logical—seemed to sneer at the love-struck creature she'd become, hit for the first time in her life by feelings that threatened to overrule everything else in her life. Every man she'd cared about in the past had only provided a mild warm-up exercise for her attraction to Evan. How could she shake free of this compelling attraction and get on with the real business of living her life as she'd planned?

When she'd lived with her parents, she vented her emotions by working in their garden. Digging in the dirt, trimming dead foliage and branches from healthy plants and helping them to thrive never failed to satisfy some basic need in her. Now she realized what was missing at Evan's otherwise lovely home; no one had bothered to plant or care for a garden for quite some time. Except for some large shrubs, trimmed more from a sense of duty than any regard for beauty, the land surrounding the house was barren. The yellowing grass screamed for bright patches of color, and Dawn found herself almost melancholy that no one had planted any flowers for Evan. A farmer couldn't be expected to use his valuable time working in a garden plot, but surely he deserved the beauty one could bring.

She wouldn't be here to plant one for him next spring, but she would never forget how tempted she was to do so.

Unable to live with her own thoughts any longer, she gathered up Gary and his truck and loaded both into her car. She was running low on some toiletries because it had seemed sensible not to buy too many things when she was not yet settled. A trip to the nearest town with a supermarket was just the distraction she needed in her overly emotional state.

On the way home she filled her gas tank and had the station attendant check under the hood. Soon she was going to need her car for a long trip; she might as well get it ready now.

Evan came in for his early-afternoon break before they returned, meeting them halfway across the yard after Dawn parked the car in the shade of the barn. The look on his face told her that he'd spent some anxious moments wondering where they were.

"You're back," he said with obvious relief, putting his arm across her shoulders and walking beside her back to the house as Gary raced ahead.

"You didn't think . . ." she began.

"That you'd left for good?"

"Evan!"

"I looked in your room. Your things were still there."

Sighing deeply, she knew she couldn't blame him. Yesterday it had certainly looked as if she planned to leave without telling him.

"I won't go without telling you," she said, keeping her eyes on the ground. "Regardless of how it looked, I was going to tell you before I left yesterday."

"But you really intended to go?"

"Yes, I think so . . . I don't know. . . . Oh, Evan, please don't ask me."

"I have to. It's not just you and me. There's Gary to consider too, you know."

"I know, and I'd never leave him alone. You know that."

"Stay until we find the proof that he's mine, Dawn."

"I don't know how I can promise that. You may never learn the truth."

"I will. The people I have working on it are good. They'll find it."

"Sooner or later," she said with resignation.

"You told me you'll be in demand in L.A. with your Spanish minor."

"You remembered that?"

"I remember everything about you."

"I won't promise, Evan. I can't. But I'll give it a little more time. The job in Maggie's department has probably been filled anyway, and there's a high turnover in my line of work."

103

"I can believe that," he said, squeezing her against his side. "Thank you, Dawn."

They ate lunch with Gary, who was much more interested in chattering about pigs and trucks than in eating his cottage cheese. Evan seemed to be enjoying the three-year-old's conversation, and Dawn felt there was something between the two of them that had been missing at first. Gary didn't seem the least bit apprehensive of Evan anymore, and his behavior was much better when he was present than it was alone with Dawn. When Evan said something in his calm, reasonable way, the little boy listened to him.

"Gary, how would you like a tractor ride after lunch?" Evan asked him.

"Isn't it too hot?" Dawn asked, feeling just a little petty for wanting to be alone with Evan herself.

"We'll only be out a few minutes. I just have to move the big one a short way, so Gary might as well come with me. Go get your hat, buddy."

"Are you coming in for a while when you bring Gary back?" she asked with a becoming flush of embarrassment.

"No, there's a little breeze, so I thought I'd play golf this afternoon."

"Oh," she said, turning her back to mask her disappointment.

"With you."

"Me?"

"You did say you love to play."

"I do, but I left my clubs with my parents."

"No problem. We can rent some at the course. I have a few things to do after I bring Gary back, but we can leave around three."

"Who will watch Gary?"

"Betty said to bring him over. If she's busy, Tammy will be more than glad to run herd on him."

"Did you even consider asking me if I wanted to play before you made arrangements for Gary?"

"I saw Betty this morning, and you weren't there to ask. I can cancel if you'd rather not play."

"You're terrible!" she said with mock anger. "Of course I'd love to play. I just don't like to feel that it's been decided without me."

Gary came running into the kitchen, ready to go, and Evan hoisted him up on his shoulders to give him a pony ride. They looked so right together that Dawn felt her throat go tight. They belonged with each other; there just had to be proof that Evan was his father. She didn't want to consider what would happen if the missing birth certificate proved that he wasn't Gary's father. Her own life was so complicated, she just didn't know how to handle a disaster like that.

Primping hadn't played much part in Dawn's life since she'd arrived at the farm; she had little time free of Gary. Now she needed a whole beauty treatment, and she used Gary's naptime to good advantage. As silly as it seemed to do her nails, give herself a facial, and trim the front of her hair just to play golf on a windy course, she wanted to look her best for Evan. This could be the last time they went anywhere together, and she wanted him to be proud of her.

"You're dumb, Dawn, dumb, dumb, dumb," she said aloud to the mirror. Had it been only days ago that she'd been fired up to climb the ladder of success, to reach the top in her field, to reform the confusing maze that passed as a welfare system in every big city in the country? Now she was wildly excited because she was going to chase a little white ball around a hot golf course with a man who could spell doom for all her plans . . . if she let him. But she couldn't. Loving Evan was becoming a fact of her existence, but she couldn't permit it to be her ruling force. Maybe they wouldn't be speaking after eighteen holes of golf, especially if she beat him. He had no idea that she was a good golfer; she'd won a few local tournaments when she was still in school and beaten more than one date who challenged her to a game. Some had resented it too.

The course wasn't crowded, and, like most of Iowa this summer, the grass was drying up from lack of water. The hardness of the fairways gave extra bounce to her drives, but she had a little trouble on the greens. They were watered regularly to keep them from dying, but they seemed faster than the plush greens in Pennsylvania. Thanks to her putting, her game wasn't her best, but she soon realized that she couldn't beat Evan on his worst day. He played superbly, just as he did everything else, and she holed her ball on the eighteenth green, wishing there was something he didn't do well.

"Great game," he said, handing her the ball.

"Great nothing! You must have me down by seven or eight strokes."

"Sweetheart, you didn't expect to beat me, did you?" he teased.

His laugh annoyed her, and she jumped to her own defense.

"I'm a good golfer. I could show you some trophies, if they weren't packed away at my parents' home."

"You don't need to convince me, honey. I can see. You're a terrific woman golfer."

"Oh!" She yanked on her clubs, but one wheel of the cart caught in a depression in the ground, making bag, cart, and all tip to the side and crash sideways.

Evan was beside her, helping her right the cart and push the clubs back into the bag, then catching her hand in his.

"I've done it again, haven't I?" he said in a tone that had the same effect on her anger as the desert sun has on an ice-cream cone.

"What can I do with you!" she said, laughing in exasperation.

"Tell me I'm the nicest male chauvinist you know, then kiss me."

"Here?"

"Anywhere, pick your spot."

"I pick a swimming pool. This state of yours is too hot."

"A swimming pool it is," he said, leading the way back to the pro shop.

"I didn't see a pool here," she said, hurrying to keep up with him.

"There isn't one."

He wouldn't say any more, even though Dawn knew they weren't heading back to the farm after they left the golf course.

"We're going toward Des Moines," she finally said when road signs plainly spelled out their destination.

"I know that."

"But what about Gary?"

"The Clatts are keeping him overnight, and Tammy will watch him at the house in the morning until we get back."

"Evan, you are crazy. I can't go anywhere looking like this."

Her new white cotton shorts had wilted on the golf course, and her navy knit top felt like it was stuck to her back.

"You can go anywhere; you look wonderful."

"In shorts I can go anywhere?"

He was enjoying his mystery so much that she let him tease her, pretending more resistance than she felt. They drove for nearly an hour and stopped at one of the nicer motels on the outskirts of the city.

"I'll only be a minute," he said, leaving the car to go into the lobby. "We have a reservation."

"Evan!" She started to protest, but he didn't stay to listen.

Their room overlooked a large, inviting indoor pool,

and Dawn looked at it longingly, in spite of her discomfort with the situation. If only she had her suit, she would swim for hours.

"You should have told me," she said, pouting. "I could have brought my swim suit."

"You did."

He opened his overnight case that he had put in the car without her knowledge and tossed her gold-patterned bikini on the bed.

"Where did you get that?"

"In your room, of course, while you were in the shower."

"You planned all of this! I suppose you brought a dress so I can go for dinner."

"No, we'll have it here. And I didn't pack your nightgown. You won't need that either."

"Evan, what is all this?" Even though his message and intent were plain, she didn't like the feeling that he expected her to go along with it.

"Just thought we needed to get away."

The only trouble is, Dawn thought with a sinking feeling, *you're the one I need to get away from.* The trap was closing around her; she felt it, and she was losing her will to resist.

The pool was wonderfully deserted, the last family group departing shortly after they arrived. Evan swam with long, powerful strokes, but Dawn didn't try to compete with him in the water. She was a poky swimmer at best, and mostly enjoyed just floating and relaxing. When he surfaced near her face, she smiled lazily.

"You owe me," he said.

"What?"

"The kiss you wouldn't give me on the golf course."

"Oh, Evan, for goodness' sake."

She kissed his cheek, intentionally missing his mouth but enjoying the coolness of his skin. Not a bit satisfied, he pulled her underwater and wrapped his legs around her. She came up sputtering and coughing, but his naughtiness had left her anything but angry.

We're playing, she thought in amazement, realizing that this was the first day they'd done anything so elementary. It had taken them all this time to reach the point where most couples begin—light-hearted courting.

Back in the room she had her choice of wearing a wet bathing suit or her less-than-fresh golfing clothes. Instead of doing either, she appropriated the clean shirt Evan had brought for himself, and dressed in it for dinner.

When their meal arrived, Dawn knew why Evan had chosen to stay in this motel; they both had magnificent lobsters, so filling that they couldn't finish the oversize baked potatoes that came with their dinners. The only thing that made the meal less enjoyable was the nagging suspicion that Evan was up to something.

They sat side by side on one of the two double beds, propped up against the headboard by mounds of pillows and sleepy from their exercise and big dinner. One situation comedy after another on the television occupied part of their attention, but both were acutely conscious of their intimacy. By unspoken mutual agreement, they touched and petted, but put off the moment when their lovemaking would begin in earnest.

"We needed this," he said softly, sliding down on the sheet to rest his head on her lap.

She wondered if his hair would turn light brown in the winter when the sun-bleached streaks fell victim to a barber's shears, and the thought that she might never know stabbed her with incredible pain.

Sensing her change in mood, he sat up and gathered her in his arms, rocking her, letting her lose herself in the protectiveness of his arms.

With rituallike formality he slowly unbuttoned the shirt she was wearing, a fine cotton sport shirt that felt silky on her skin. Pushing it from her shoulders, he kissed the smooth skin that lay bare to his touch and more impatiently loosened the clasp of her bra and discarded it. Instead of the expected flood of feeling when his hands cupped her breasts, she felt her body go rigid. When he bent his head to moisten the hard tips with his tongue, she pulled away without reason, not understanding her own reluctance to embark on the road to sensual surrender. Her body gave the familiar signs of willingness as a hot, tight feeling stabbed at her loins, but her mind rejected the relief he could give her.

It should have been the best of times for them, but something was dreadfully wrong. The more he demanded of her, the more she held back, until, in the end, only the mechanics remained. They turned away from each other to try to sleep, the space between them like a chasm.

For Dawn the night was a hundred hours long. When she did doze, her dreams were disturbing, making it seem as if she spent the whole night trying not to wake Evan with her restlessness. When staying in bed became unbearable, she eased away from him and fumbled to dress in the dark.

Even the earliest risers weren't up when she left the room, but she had to be alone with her thoughts for a while. Outside, the sky was a murky gray, with just enough light so she could see. The only trouble was that she couldn't imagine less congenial territory for taking a walk. She could circle the motel, which mostly involved walking through the parking areas, or she could walk along the busy, commercial highway. Had she reached the point in life where she couldn't even go for a walk successfully?

The dining room wasn't open yet, but there was nothing to stop her from sitting in the deserted lobby, nothing, that is, except that she felt like a hobo hanging around in her rumpled golf clothes. When she caught a glimpse of herself in a mirror, she was struck by the irony of her situation.

I'm wallowing in self-pity, she thought, *feeling sorry for myself. I've always dreamed that someday a real man would make love to me, and now that it's happened, I want to go back to being a little girl, absorbed in my own interests, unhampered by the responsibilities of love.*

She remembered her plans for her sixth birthday; her mother had told her to choose between a party with her friends or dinner in a restaurant with her parents. Wanting both, she threw her first and last leg-kicking, breath-holding, eardrum-shattering temper tantrum, with the result that both plans were scrapped. She had spent a lonely day at home, sulking.

"I must be crazy," she said aloud as she hurried back to the room. Evan had given her a wonderful no-strings-attached affair, something she'd never forget, and she was pouting because she couldn't be in two places at once.

Of course, she was going to make it to California, and if she lost one job opportunity, there would be others. Social work was a wide-open field, and she had the drive and will to succeed. When she left, she'd take with her memories of a wonderful, magical experience, not sadness and regret because Evan's world wasn't the one she wanted.

In her haste to get off by herself, she'd forgotten to take a room key. One soft tap was all it took to send the door flying inward.

"Where the devil were you?" Evan asked, standing before her, fully dressed. "I was just going out to look for you."

"Kiss me good morning, then yell at me," she said, standing on tiptoe to give him aid and encouragement.

"Kiss you! You deserve a good spanking, not a kiss. Where've you been at this time of the morning? It isn't even light."

111

"For goodness' sake, Evan, you don't own me! I couldn't sleep anymore, so I walked around a little."

"It's five in the morning."

"Much too early to be out of bed, I agree."

Casually, as though she took early dawn walks every day, she stripped off all her clothes.

"Come here," she invited him.

"I don't know, Dawn."

She'd never heard him sound so puzzled, and it suited her new mood perfectly. Perspective was what they both needed; they were healthy, vigorous, energetic adults. It was natural that they find each other attractive. That didn't mean he would sell his farm for her, or that she should scrap all her ambitions for him. Maybe, after she was resettled, they'd visit each other and renew their pleasurable acquaintance.

This is what she thought until he was beside her, drawing her against him with a hunger that was far from one-sided. As much as she would have liked to go on pretending, this wasn't a casual game they were playing.

"I've never met anyone like you," he said.

"It feels so good when you hold me," she whispered, completely forgetting that she was going to act like a sophisticated woman.

"Why did you leave?"

"I just needed time to think."

"About what?"

"You'll think it's silly," she said, snuggling even closer and feeling electrical currents building between them.

"Try me."

He slipped one leg between hers, moving it slowly and teasingly, his hands pressed on the base of her spine.

"I can't keep my mind on talking if you do that," she said with a faint laugh.

"Then I won't distract you."

He moved away, leaving her with a deserted feeling.

"I want to be distracted."

"Do you?"

He leaned over her on one elbow, the intensity of his stare making her blink her eyes.

"Hold me again," she begged.

"First tell me what mysterious thoughts sent you prowling."

"Nothing really. I was thinking about my sixth birthday. I had a temper tantrum because I couldn't have a party and go to a restaurant too."

"That's what you were thinking about?" His laugh was a little skeptical. "Which did you do?"

"Neither. My father got so mad that I had to stay home alone."

"And staying home was a punishment. So what you were really thinking about was losing things you want?"

"Yes, I guess so. Is this important now, Evan?"

He drew in his breath sharply. "No, I guess it really isn't."

She felt his mind slipping away from her and couldn't bear it. With a quick, convulsive movement she wrapped her arms around him, clinging to his torso with all her strength.

"You are something else," he said, bringing his lips down to graze hers lightly.

With a sharp little cry she rejected his offer of tenderness and captured his lips with her teeth, passionately gnawing until he retaliated.

Craving physical sensations, she demanded them. In her mind she imagined a schoolroom blackboard with no white chalk lines marring it. Concentrating on this image, she forced her mind to become blank, so no disturbing thoughts could dull her sensitivities or lessen her responsiveness. She imagined herself as an unformed mound of clay, and only Evan's touch gave her shape and substance. When he outlined the shape of her body with his hard

113

hands and soft kisses, she became a living mass again, straining to be part of him.

His body was hard, but not unyielding, as she groped for the contacts that would make him wholly hers. Aroused by her uninhibited responses, he forgot the evening before for the moment, throwing aside his role as the tender, gentle lover and meeting her eagerness with unrestrained enthusiasm. Locked in the lover's knot, they abandoned themselves to the pounding of their heartbeats and the high they were building.

There was sorrow at the peak of their lovemaking, sadness that perfect moments are so fleeting and so hard to recapture. Both were sure at that moment that this was the happiest, most complete moment of their lives. Reluctant to let go of bliss, they clung together, trading weak kisses and tiny gestures of caring.

"I don't think I really know you," Evan said, almost to himself.

Not understanding what he meant, Dawn only snuggled closer.

They dozed, then tried to recapture the heights of longing again; fatigue made them more gentle, but not less caring, until they both had to surface to the world of reality.

While Dawn showered, Evan ordered a mammoth breakfast that seemed to include a sampling of the entire menu. She laughed when she saw it, but he was the one who laughed at the tremendous appetite she had. Unbelievably, they nearly devoured it all—scrambled eggs, fried potatoes, bacon, hot muffins with honey and jam, crisp whole-wheat toast, fresh melon, and a jug of dark aromatic coffee. Leaning back in the cushioned chairs, they both felt as though their appetites had been sated for life.

The morning was nearly gone when they finished checking out, and Evan seemed both edgy and remote. Dawn blamed it on his eagerness to get back to the farm, and he did push his luck all the way there, driving in excess of the rigidly enforced speed limit but escaping the notice of the highway patrol.

Back at the house everything was normal and familiar, but Dawn felt as if she were viewing it from another dimension. She needed time to assimilate what had happened, but the day's routine came rushing at her. Urging Gary to pick up his toys, preparing his lunch, thawing something for dinner—all of these were so commonplace that she couldn't believe she was the same person who, only hours earlier, had thrown all restraints to the wind to give herself totally to a man. Surely that love-crazed couple had been two other people.

Evan came in to have dinner with them, but turned down her suggestion that they take Gary into town to see a movie.

"I have twenty-four hours of paperwork I have to handle tonight," he said. "Do me a favor and make me a big pot of coffee. You can put it in that thermos pitcher."

Dawn went to bed while he was still working in his office and woke up in the early morning, alone in her bed. She was more than a little stiff from all the exercise the day before and not at all inclined to feel amorous, but it would have been nice to have Evan beside her, just to talk a little and kiss good morning and . . . just to be there.

After putting on her robe and slippers, she went looking for him and found him fixing his own breakfast.

"I can do that for you," she offered sleepily.

"No need. I'm used to it. Coffee?"

"Please. Sit down, and I'll watch your eggs."

"Okay," he said, "if you like."

Why had he had so little to say to her since they'd returned from the motel? It made Dawn uneasy, but she couldn't put her finger on any real reason.

He ate rapidly, and she followed him through the family room on his way out to the barn.

"Evan," she said abruptly, then realized she didn't know what she wanted to say to him.

"What? I have to go to work, Dawn."

"Oh, nothing, I guess. Will you be back for lunch?"

"Better not plan on it. I have to run over and get that part I ordered."

"Gary and I could ride along."

" 'Fraid not. I won't have time to come back here for you. I'll see you at dinner."

"Well, have a good day."

"You too."

He left quickly with no smile, no good-bye kiss, no promise in his eyes. Dawn felt desolate, yet she couldn't define what it was she wanted from him. He knew she'd be leaving soon; she knew it too. What was there for them to talk about?

No amount of rationalization made her day seem less empty. Even though she dutifully cared for Gary and tried to keep him entertained, her whole day seemed so pointless. What was she doing here, marooned on a farm in Iowa and feeling crushed because its owner hadn't kissed her good-bye that morning? She wanted to disentangle herself from Evan Crane's life, and now that he was making it easier for her, she was miserable.

The answer that was forming in her mind only led her into a maze of new torments. Selfishly, she'd only considered what her love for Evan meant in her life. Loving him so much that she even flirted with the idea of staying with him, she hadn't faced one chilling fact. Evan had never even hinted that he wanted her to stay on. He needed her until he was sure Gary was his son, but beyond that he never suggested that he wanted her in his life. His coldness had to be his way of letting her know that there wasn't any future for them together.

If Evan didn't feel any love at all for her, then the dilemma of whether to leave him was resolved. She really was free to go wherever she pleased whenever she pleased. Relieved of the necessity of making a decision, she should have been light-hearted with relief. Instead she was miserable.

Dinner wasn't quiet; Gary kept them entertained with his insatiable curiosity. Still, Evan and Dawn managed to say very little of any importance to each other. After they exhausted Gary's antics as a topic of conversation, neither of them made any personal comments. It was as if they were two total strangers who were politely tolerating each other. For Dawn it hurt like the devil. Was this her punishment for giving herself so completely to a man she didn't plan to cherish forever?

Again Evan retreated to his office, complaining that the paperwork was by far the most tedious part of running the farm. Dawn played outside with Gary, even though she didn't feel like dousing herself with insect repellent and getting spruce needles in her hair, then she put him to bed when he'd used up his energy supply for the day.

Poking as much as possible, she took a leisurely bath, washed a few clothing items by hand, did her nails, and straightened her already neat room. Tonight she had no intention of going to bed until the lion came out of his lair, so to speak, but keeping busy until Evan stopped working wasn't going to be easy. She sat through a television show, but she couldn't concentrate on it.

When her restless pacing threatened to wear a path in the family-room carpet, she decided to check on Evan. She could offer him some coffee or a piece of plum cake left from dinner; certainly he wouldn't resent such a friendly interruption.

Her knock was soft, but she couldn't believe he hadn't heard it. When she pounded the door more forcefully with her knuckles, making them smart in the process, there was

117

still no response. The crack under the door showed that a light was still on in the office, so it was unlikely that Evan had gone to bed.

More than a little nervous, she eased the door open a crack. Evan was seated in his chair, the only one in the room, and the desk was littered with papers and ledgers. In spite of the businesslike look of the room, he wasn't working. His chair was turned toward a window, and he was slumped back, motionless.

"Would you like a snack, Evan? There's some plum cake left."

"No, thanks."

"Some coffee maybe?"

"No, Dawn, nothing."

His words were so stern that she felt he was rejecting her, not her offer.

"I just thought you might like something."

"Coffee, cake, or a roll in the hay?" He stood up and glared at her.

"That's nasty!" she protested, stung by the tone of his voice.

Yesterday morning had been so wonderful for both of them. What could possibly have happened to make him so distant and mean?

"It was meant to be."

"Evan, what's wrong with you?"

She pushed the door shut behind her but made no move to come closer to him.

"I've just been doing a lot of thinking," he said wearily.

"Well, it doesn't seem to agree with you."

"But that isn't your worry, is it, Dawn? I'm not one of your case histories. Or am I? Will this go into your files as a classic father-discovers-unknown-son case?"

"I don't deserve that," she said.

"What do you deserve? A commendation for handling Gary's case so well? When you write up your notes, don't forget to mention that you had to play house to pull off this big reunion."

"It's nothing like that," she cried out in despair, running from the room with barely suppressed tears fighting for release.

She made it to her room, but he was right behind her, preventing her from locking the door by filling it with his body.

"What do you expect of me, Dawn?"

"Leave me alone!"

"That's what I was doing. You came to my office, remember?"

"Why have you changed like this?" Her voice was choked with anger and frustration.

He came into the room and closed the door but kept his distance from her.

"I told you. I've been thinking."

"About what?"

"Mostly I wonder about the night in the motel, Dawn. Why didn't it work between us then?"

"Everything was fine in the morning."

"I'm not so sure it was, but I'm not talking about the morning. What was keeping us apart the night before?"

"You got what you wanted then too," she said defensively.

"And what was that?"

"Sex," she said bitterly.

"Lousy sex. Your mind was a million miles away. You made me feel like I'd blackmailed you into being there."

"I never intended to."

"I don't know what your intentions were."

"Evan, I was uneasy . . ."

"About what, for God's sake? You should have known by then that I wasn't going to make you do anything you didn't want to."

"It wasn't that!"

119

"What, then?" he exploded. "You made me feel like I was forcing myself on you."

"I didn't!"

"Oh, what difference does it make?" He sounded older and defeated.

"Evan, I didn't know why you'd brought me to the motel, why it had to be such a big mystery. I have things on my mind too, like missing out on a great job opportunity. I just wasn't ready for surprises."

"And that's my fault," he said with obvious self-blame.

"Yes—and no. Oh, Evan, what was the big mystery about going to the motel? You have no idea how uneasy it made me."

"Forget it."

"No, tell me why you brought me there," she demanded.

"To ask you a question in a place where the phone wouldn't ring and Gary wouldn't pop in on us."

There could be only one question that important, and Dawn felt herself go rigid, the same way she had in the motel room that evening.

When she said nothing, he asked, "Don't you want to know what the question was?"

She shook her head. "Please, just leave me alone, Evan."

"No, you want to know. I brought you there to ask you to marry me, Dawn."

"But you didn't ask," she said wretchedly.

"You gave me your answer."

It wasn't surprise that she felt; from the moment Evan had sprung the motel on her, she'd known that he was planning something. There was only one thing she didn't understand.

"In the morning, why didn't you ask me then?"

"It was too late, Dawn."

He thrust both hands into his pants pockets and

hunched his shoulders, making her feel desperately protective toward him. Somehow she had hurt him deeply, but how could he overlook their wonderful morning together?

"Evan, it was good for both of us in the morning, wasn't it?"

"Terrific," he said with irony, "but it didn't have anything to do with the till death do us part bit, did it?"

"I don't know what to say," she said miserably, her hands balled into rigid fists.

"You don't have to say anything. Face it, Dawn, I'm not great husband material. Peg made that clear enough. I come with nine hundred acres of responsibility, and all I can guarantee are long workdays, the possibility of bad years when the harvest fails or the bottom falls out of farm prices, and the monotony of being home alone a lot. Is that a package you're going to jump at?"

"Please don't put things that way, Evan."

"If I get down on my knees and propose in the best Victorian tradition, will it change anything?"

"No, but—"

"Will it make you give up your harebrained ideas about saving the world in California?"

"You have no right to say that! I take my work just as seriously as you take yours."

"Then I was right, your answer would have been no."

"You'll never know, because you didn't ask!"

She was so angry, she could see him only through a red haze. Why couldn't this be a simple boy-meets-girl situation, so she could fall into his arms and live happily ever after?

"All right, I'll ask," he snapped back, sounding just as angry as she felt. "Will you marry me?"

"Oh, you're safe in asking now, because I'm so mad I wouldn't have you if you were the king of England."

"Then why provoke me into asking?" he yelled.

"I didn't provoke you! The only thing I want is to get away from you as soon as possible!"

"You have your keys. Leave! But don't you dare take Gary with you, or I'll have the state police on your trail before you reach the county line."

"I wouldn't take your son."

"The boy you, and you alone, assume is my son!"

"Evan," she said, panicking, "what will you do if you never find his birth records? What if you find them, and he isn't yours?"

"That's when you'd better be here to pick up the pieces," he said cruelly. "Don't ever forget that you started this."

"I don't understand you! How can you be so cold and uncaring, as if a piece of paper was the all-important thing in the world?"

"You told me before that a piece of paper doesn't mean much, didn't you?"

He moved closer, stalking her with eyes made a brilliant green by the intensity of his anger. Backing away, she was trapped by the bed on one side and the wall on the other, and she just wouldn't give him the satisfaction of seeing her crawl across the bed to get away from him.

His face was only inches from hers, and his eyes held her mesmerized, penetrating hers without revealing his intent. Her hands went up instinctively, as though to ward off a blow, but his violence took another turn. Crushing her against him, he attacked, fastening his mouth over hers with unmerciful force, bruising her lips while he buried his fingers in her hair, clutching her scalp until she thought her skull would shatter.

With the bed behind her knees, she fell back easily when he released her, making her fully vulnerable to whatever he intended. Motionless, he only stared at her.

His face lost all trace of animation, but his eyes burned into hers. For a long instant he towered over her, frozen in his pose of rage. Then the self-control she'd marveled at before seemed to take possession of him, and she made a tiny, involuntary gesture of invitation, touching her breasts lightly with trembling fingers.

"It will be much easier for both of us," he said hoarsely, "if we stop playing games. You stay in your bed, and I'll stay in mine. Hopefully I won't need to inconvenience you much longer."

"Inconvenience," she repeated, sounding stupid in her own ears. "What you've been doing to me isn't even related to inconvenience."

"I'm tired," he said truthfully enough. "Keep both of your doors locked. That way you'll know I won't disturb you again."

She knew it anyway. The note of finality in his voice tore her to ribbons. She'd made an enemy of Evan Crane, the last man in the world she wanted to cast in that role.

Lying back on the bed, she tried to will away the pain, but nothing worked, not pretending her whole body was a piece of limp spaghetti or imagining that her limbs were weighed down with concrete, the two relaxing techniques that worked most often for her. Even though she breathed deeply and massaged her throbbing temples, she felt frozen into one lump of misery.

How could Evan do this to her when she cared so much about him? Wasn't there any way their minds could mesh the way their bodies had? Tears didn't come, but neither did sleep. It was the longest night of her life, and she hoped Evan felt as confused and desolate as she did.

CHAPTER SEVEN

In the early hours of the morning Dawn finally managed to sink into a restless doze, but when Gary invaded her room and climbed on the bed beside her, it felt as if she hadn't slept at all. His energy made her feel like an ancient crone too feeble to get her feet on the floor, but, prompted by his insistence, she did make the effort. At least she didn't need to worry about meeting Evan; it was long past his usual awakening time, and he was sure to be working.

When she found Mrs. Winsch cleaning the oven, Dawn was embarrassed to look like such a sluggard, still wearing her robe and trying to shake off her sleepiness. Mrs. Winsch didn't seem to notice, but her cheerfulness was a reproach in its own way; it made Dawn feel like a grouch.

"If Gary or you have any dirty clothes, just drop them down the chute. No trouble to do them up with Mr. Crane's," she said after giving Gary a warm good-morning hug.

"Gary may have a few things. I'll check his room," Dawn said, glad for an excuse to leave the room.

Gary enjoyed Mrs. Winsch's company immensely, a mutual feeling that still gave Dawn hope that the woman might consider full-time work if Gary's welfare was involved. Gary's play clothes from the day before were lying on a chair, so she deposited them in the hall laundry chute, but she didn't even check her own laundry bag hanging in her closet, half full of dirty clothes. The way she felt this

124

morning, she didn't even want her laundry mingling in the same wash load with Evan's. He couldn't have told her more plainly that their lives were to be totally separate. For the few more days she needed to stay because of Gary, her emotional survival would depend on keeping her distance.

Shampooing her hair under a moderate spray, she couldn't help but notice that the sliding door was still wet from Evan's shower earlier that morning. How unlike him not to wipe up after himself. Was Mr. Neatness just a little off his stride? Gloating over this thought, she got a glob of burning shampoo in her eye. She left the bathroom as quickly as possible, shutting the door so the faint fragrance of his after-shave didn't escape into her room. Why did he need to smell nice to work on a farm? It stung a little to realize that she didn't really know what he did or whom he saw during the day.

She dressed rapidly in faded jeans and a red halter that was more cheerful-looking than she felt. Even though Gary was with Mrs. Winsch and more than likely to follow her around for hours, Dawn had things to do. Particularly there was an important phone call that she had to make, and she wanted to catch Cliff Harding before he went to court or became tied up with clients. If the attorney knew anything about Gary's status, she had a right to know too, and she absolutely could not go to Evan for information.

At exactly nine o'clock she punched out Cliff's number on Evan's office phone, but her timing wasn't successful. He was in conference with a client, and the best his secretary would promise was that she'd try to have him return the call before noon.

Hoping to catch the return call in the privacy of Evan's office before he returned to the house, she decided to type additional copies of her job résumé. It wouldn't hurt to have more in reserve if she needed them. His electric

125

typewriter made sharp, professional-looking copy, and it also gave her a perfect excuse for being in his office. She told Mrs. Winsch where she'd be and why, then settled down to type.

The mechanical act of transferring words from one paper to another was just the kind of job she needed. With her mediocre typing skills she had to concentrate too hard to think about anything else. More copies than she was likely to need were stacked in a pile, and it was uncomfortably close to noon before the call finally came.

"Dawn, Cliff Harding here. My secretary gave me your message to call."

"Oh, thank you for calling me back, Cliff. I need to know what progress has been made in finding Gary's birth records. Maybe Sheila has some family who would help, if she won't. What is Evan doing about her letter?"

"Well . . ." He hesitated. "There is one small problem, I'm afraid, Dawn. Evan is my client, and it's not ethical for me to give the information to anyone but him. I'm anxious to help you, of course, but my hands are tied. You understand professional ethics, I'm sure, being a professional person yourself."

Ignoring his obvious appeal to her ego, she was determined to push the issue.

"All I need to know is when you'll be able to confirm Gary's birth. Couldn't you give me a progress report without betraying your client? Cliff, it's terribly important to me to know that Gary will have a home."

"Now, don't sound so worried, Dawn. I hired a good agency for the job, one I've used many times before. I'm confident they'll get results soon, very soon."

"Cliff, what if Gary isn't Evan's son? What will happen to him then?"

"I'm awfully sorry, Dawn. I just can't answer that one either. I assume we'd have to involve the courts in that case. You might have to meet with Evan and me to help

126

work out a solution, so you will keep yourself available, won't you?"

"Do you think Gary will have to become a ward of the state?" she asked, alarmed, even though the lawyer could only confirm what she suspected herself. "There could be all kinds of sticky problems if the birth record can't be located," she added.

"Let's just say it's an outside possibility and not something to worry about until the time comes," he said in a patronizing voice that only irritated her. "Say, how long is Evan going to keep you down on the farm? I'm still looking forward to our luncheon date."

"Things are a little hectic now, Cliff, but thank you anyway. I'd appreciate anything you can do to resolve this more quickly."

"Just relax and let me do the worrying. Uncle Cliff is giving it his best shot, sweetheart."

Dawn cringed when he used the endearment but managed to break off the call, sounding grateful for his efforts. If she could believe the lawyer, and Evan seemed to think he was trustworthy and capable, then the waiting period should be nearly over. Perhaps in just a few days she would be on her way to California with the knowledge that she'd succeeded in her goal of securing a home for Gary. At least she'd have that satisfaction to take away with her.

Taking advantage of Mrs. Winsch's obvious fondness for Gary, Dawn left him in her charge, changed her clothes as quickly as possible, and left the house before Evan could be expected to return. If he came back to the house while both she and the housekeeper were there, it would be so awkward. Sharp-eyed and interested in people, Mrs. Winsch was sure to notice the hostility between her employer and his house guest, so the easiest thing was to leave for a while. Driving aimlessly, Dawn finally came to a small town with a two-block business district and a grain elevator. None of the buildings had been modernized in Dawn's lifetime, and the drugstore had an old-fashioned soda fountain with syrup in pumps and a root-beer barrel. She indulged in a hot-fudge sundae with whipped cream and nuts, served in a pedestaled glass dish, and called it her lunch, topping it off with a root beer in a frosted mug. Once her favorite sticky concoction would have soothed her hurt feelings and given her at least an imaginary lift, but sweets were no panacea for the way she felt now. She left the store feeling slightly nauseated from the overdose of rich food on an empty stomach.

Once the town had boasted about its fine theater and had drawn customers from all over the county, but now the marquee was blank and the windows boarded up, television and fast transportation to a larger city having doomed the rural entertainment center. Dawn wandered past it, regretting its demise and particularly wishing that she could kill time this afternoon by sitting inside a dark theater lost in an absorbing melodrama. She'd never gone to a movie alone, but today was the day for it.

For lack of anything better to do, she drove aimlessly over roads that were monotonously similar, finally managing to lose herself very thoroughly. It took a young but patient service station attendant at a rural crossroads nearly five minutes to figure out where she wanted to go and give her directions to get back to Evan's farm.

Besides killing time, she'd accomplished nothing. Going over and over everything that had happened between them since the golf game only made her feel more frustrated and less in control. She had been uneasy when Evan took her to the motel; it was obvious that he had something special in mind, and she'd known in her heart that he wanted to define and possibly cement their relationship. If they'd parted in anger after her frigid response that evening, she would be able to understand his feelings better. The next morning had seemed to bring them together again, but Evan didn't see it that way. Maybe because the damage had already been done, he hadn't felt the same specialness she'd experienced when they made love at dawn. She'd made the woman's age-old error in mistaking a man's physical response for total involvement, and recognizing it didn't make it hurt less. Was there anything she could do to restore what they had had? Could she beg him to let her stay with him forever? She knew she couldn't. But wasn't there any alternative, any way that they could preserve some of the wonder they'd experienced in first discovering each other?

Betty Clatt had warned her that Evan was a "forever" person, but Dawn wasn't sure how she felt about it. Certainly she'd dreamed of having a husband and children someday, but she always saw a family as something that would come after she proved herself out in the world. She didn't want to be a woman who woke up at the age of forty to discover she'd blown all her potential. Now that she'd fallen in love, she wondered if her judgment was sophomoric and her plans backward. The worst thing Evan had done to her was to make her doubt her own goals. He'd made her life so complicated! Why couldn't he have said "Welcome, Son" without all this fuss about proof? Then Dawn could have left before her emotions became so entangled.

Engrossed in thought, she made a wrong turn going back to the farm, but fortunately a man just bringing in his mail gave her new directions when she stopped. She arrived at the house with an hour to spare before Mrs. Winsch had to leave, but her afternoon alone hadn't been pleasant or refreshing. Thinking through her situation had only left her more confused and miserable.

Mrs. Winsch's corned beef and cabbage defied the best efforts of the air-conditioner to dispel its aroma, and Dawn served it promptly at six o'clock, even though Evan wasn't there. She couldn't be expected to delay dinner for a man who didn't tell her his schedule. His portion could stay until it dried to the consistency of leather, for all she cared, but she did dish out a generous serving, covering it with foil before returning it to the oven.

Gary saw Evan first and climbed down from his chair to greet him, but Dawn sat motionless, refusing to be the first to speak. The food in her mouth turned to sawdust, but she forced herself to swallow, keeping her eyes averted.

"Is my dinner in the oven?" he asked curtly.

"Look, if you want to know. Gary, get back on your chair."

Instead of obeying her, Gary watched Evan take his covered plate out of the oven and turn off the heat.

"Gary, sit down," she said sharply, looking at the pair of them.

"Don't use him for target practice," Evan said, coming within full range of her glare for the first time since returning.

"What happened to your hand?" she asked, trying to mask her concern over the bulky white bandage he was wearing with a cold, matter-of-fact tone.

"Just an accident."

"I didn't think you bandaged your hand for decoration."

"Sarcasm doesn't become you."

"I asked a simple question; you could have the courtesy to reply."

"I punctured it trying to replace the tractor part I just picked up."

"Is it bad?"

"Bad enough to go to the emergency room for stitches and a tetanus shot," he said gruffly as he put the hot plate on the table with his uninjured hand.

Looking into his face for the first time, she couldn't help but notice how drawn and tired he looked. Dark circles shadowed his eyes, and without his healthy tan, he would have looked haggard.

"You look terrible. Did it bleed much?" she asked, struggling to keep her voice impersonal.

"Enough."

He ate mechanically, but her meal had ended the moment he returned. Even Gary was unusually quiet, fascinated by Evan's bandage but not nearly so vocal as usual. He played with his food, making a mess on the table, but Dawn refused to correct him. If Evan wanted his son to have good table manners, let him do something about them.

"If anyone wants me, I'll be in my office," he said after hurriedly eating most of the food Dawn had put aside for him.

"Shouldn't you lie down for a while? Maybe you lost more blood than you realize."

"Your concern is touching," he said, sarcastic himself now, "but I don't need any mothering."

Flushing angrily, she tried to think of a searing reply but failed. He was so maddening that he left her without adequate words.

Gary was naughty all evening, pulling pans from the kitchen cupboards while she tried to clean up and tearing through the house like a banshee. The only miracle was that Evan didn't leave his office to complain about the uproar. Getting the rowdy little boy to bed made Dawn feel as if she'd accomplished at least something that day. She understood why the welfare mothers she'd worked with complained that their toddlers were driving them crazy.

She heard the phone ring over the dull drone of the TV, but Evan picked it up in his office before she could reach the kitchen extension.

"The phone is for you," he said, coming into the family room. "You can take it in my office."

131

"I can use the kitchen phone."

"Use my office. I'm going to bed," he said.

The only people who knew where she was were her parents and Maggie, and she didn't feel like talking to any of them. She closed the office door behind her and picked up the receiver with misgivings, wondering what possible excuse she could give for lingering in Iowa so long.

"Dawn, it's Maggie," her friend said in a voice less cheerful than usual.

"Let me guess," Dawn said pessimistically. "Your boss hired someone else for the job."

"Well, yes, I'm afraid he did. I did try to warn you, Dawn, that he had a lot of good candidates for the job. It would have been great, though, having you in the same department."

"Well, there will be other opportunities, I'm sure. I can't leave Gary until the situation here is resolved, but the detectives should come up with something soon. The attorney assured me they would."

"Dawn, there must be baby-sitters available. Are you sure it's Gary you can't leave?"

"Absolutely sure."

"Well, don't sound so mad; I only asked. About another job—"

"You have another lead?" Dawn interrupted, wondering why she didn't feel the loss of the one in Maggie's department more keenly.

"Well, no, things are a little tighter than usual with our budget cuts and all, but it's really not the job I called about."

"Did you get my check for my share of next month's rent?"

"Yes, but, you see, something has come up."

Maggie sounded miserable, but Dawn wasn't in any mood to make it easy for her if she had more bad news to spring.

"It shouldn't be too long now, Maggie. I talked to the lawyer who's handling Gary's investigation just this morning. He sounded optimistic."

"Dawn, hold it. I have to tell you something. Remember I wrote you last winter that I was going with someone, then he moved to Seattle?"

"Yes, I remember."

"Well, he transferred back, not because he got a better job, but because he missed me. What I'm trying to say, Maggie, is that we're going to give our relationship a serious try. Instead of hunting for an apartment and all, Brad is going to stay with me."

"Live with you?"

"Well, actually, yes. The way we're thinking now, we'll get married in the fall, so there wouldn't be any point in having two apartments on our hands. You have to sign a lease to get anything at all decent out here. Dawn, you don't know how bad I feel. I promised you a place to stay; I even talked you into coming. But I still plan to help you. You can sleep on our couch when you first get here, and I'm asking all through the department to see if anyone is looking for a roommate. I'll do everything I can to help you get settled, I promise."

Dawn could almost feel Maggie squirming with guilt, so her first instinct was to make it as easy as possible for her friend. Part of her sympathized with Maggie; after all, love was something that didn't come along very often. Yet her own letdown kept her silent for a long, uncomfortable moment.

"I'm a lousy roommate anyway; I have to tell you the truth," Maggie babbled nervously. "Brad's threatened to turn me over his knee if I leave the air-conditioner set at sixty-five degrees again, and I haven't cleaned the fridge since I moved in. I'm afraid something in there will grab me and eat me, it's been that long."

Apparently Brad had moved in already, and Dawn

wondered how long it had taken Maggie to build up enough courage to call her. The only thing that angered her was that the whole move had been Maggie's suggestion to begin with.

"It's okay, Maggie," she said woodenly, wondering why she didn't feel disappointment or any of the other things she should be feeling. The bottom had just dropped out of her plans, and she didn't seem to care.

"No, it's not okay! I feel awful," her friend wailed. "I was the one who got you all excited about L.A., and now I'm letting you down. I do want you to be in my wedding, though, if you can ever forgive me."

"You're forgiven, silly. I'm delighted for you."

"Oh, Dawn, I hope you mean that!"

"Of course I do," she said, trying to sound as enthusiastic as possible. "It's wonderful that you're getting together with Brad. I know how much you hated to see him leave L.A."

"And you will stay with us when you get here?" Maggie insisted.

"When I get there," Dawn assured her, knowing in her heart that she would never be the third person in Maggie's apartment or a bridesmaid in her wedding. She just didn't care anymore if she never saw California. Maggie's call only made her admit it to herself. The only thing she really wanted right now was to go home and be petted and loved by her adoring parents. They would be overjoyed that she wasn't moving so far from them, and her long fight to assert her independence would be over. It didn't even matter that she'd lost.

Evan's door was shut when she passed it, but she hadn't expected anything else. One thing was absolutely certain —her destination when she left Iowa was none of his concern. She didn't intend to tell him that her plans to go to California had all gone sour.

She locked her door, then got out of bed and unlocked

it. She had shut Evan out when he sensed her withdrawal in the motel room; he wouldn't try her door again. Only Gary would be kept away, and she felt her responsibility for the child too keenly to lock him out.

The summer heat was the worst in years, keeping Gary confined to the house most of the day, but it didn't stop Evan from leaving the house early and returning only when the evening became too dark for work. Dawn wondered where he ate, if he ate at all, and in spite of her determination to put him out of her life, she worried about his health. When she did catch a glimpse of him, he looked totally beat.

For three days he asked only one thing of her, that she rebandage his hand, a job he found nearly impossible to do himself, since it was his right hand that was hurt. She did the job gently and carefully, peeling off the soiled gauze and washing his hand around the wound, but it was disturbing to her to see the angry redness around the stitches.

"You should have a doctor look at this," she warned, dabbing on some medication that didn't seem to be helping at all.

"It will be okay," he said gruffly, but he finally promised to stop at his doctor's office that afternoon.

The closeness necessary to replace the bandage made them both uncomfortable, but at least he heeded her advice. Dawn knew he'd seen a doctor because his hand was bandaged much more professionally when he came home late that night. He didn't mention it to her, however, and the wall of silence between them kept getting thicker and thicker.

She awoke in the morning, knowing that something was different; there was a heaviness in the atmosphere that was both threatening and oppressive. Going to the window, she sniffed the air apprehensively and saw the heavy black

135

storm clouds gathering over the fields. The air was absolutely still with not a leaf or stalk showing any motion, a condition unusual in this prairie state where the wind blew almost every day, even when it was blast-furnace hot.

After dressing hastily, she went to see if Evan was still in the house and found him checking out the weather forecast on the kitchen radio.

"We're in for a storm," he said matter-of-factly.

"I guessed as much."

"Don't let Gary outside this morning. It sounds like it might be a big blow."

"I do have some common sense."

"When you choose to use it maybe."

"I can see you don't want company for breakfast!"

"I've had breakfast," he said.

She flounced off, wondering why the sparks started to fly every time they were in the same room, which wasn't often. Evan spent only enough time in the house to satisfy his basic need for sleep and to keep his paperwork under control. Not even Gary could commandeer more than a few minutes of his time every day, although Evan was almost affectionate with the little boy now, the only good thing that had happened since she'd come there.

Evan disappeared into his office, and Gary woke up ready for action. By noon the situation was much the same; Evan was still closeted in his office, and the sky was blacker than ever but hadn't released any much-needed rain. Before she could ask him if he wanted lunch with Gary, Evan came out and told her to fix him a sandwich.

"I'm not your housekeeper," she snapped, surprised at the depth of her own feeling.

His demand made her feel like an unpaid hired girl or a wife of thirty years, she wasn't sure which. The only reason she was there at all was that she couldn't bring herself to leave Gary until his relationship with Evan was

136

legally established. Waiting on Evan Crane wasn't her responsibility.

"No, you're not," he said angrily, and went into the kitchen to fix his own lunch.

Gary went into the kitchen to join him, but Dawn preferred hunger to being in Evan's company. She heard the low hum of the radio coming from the kitchen and an occasional burst of laughter that showed the two were enjoying their meal, making her feel left out.

"Dawn, get down to the basement!" Evan was in the doorway with Gary in one arm, calling furiously to her.

"What?"

"There's a tornado in the area."

He grabbed her arm, wincing as his sore hand made contact, and pulled her toward the basement door.

"I'm coming," she said, impatiently shaking off his grip. "Move it."

He pushed her ahead, and she ran of her own accord; his urgent warning definitely had frightened her. She dashed down the stairs, then looked to him for directions.

"In that corner," he said, pointing toward the recreation area. "Hold Gary. I'll get the radio on my workbench so we know what's going on."

Evan hadn't exaggerated. Urgent warnings came from the nearest station, and Dawn knew the area well enough now to know that the tornado had been sighted within a few miles of where they were.

The frantic dash to the basement made Gary a double handful, and he refused to be entertained or quieted. He climbed all over Dawn, one rubber-soled shoe jabbing painfully into her stomach.

"Gary, settle down," she said emphatically.

"Just because you're nervous, don't yell at Gary," Evan said.

"I'm not nervous. I'm angry because he just gave me a

137

kick that really hurt. *You* hold him if you think I'm over-reacting."

"It's what you do best, isn't it? That and causing trouble?"

She lifted Gary up and away from her and rushed out, preferring the tornado to the violent eruption of her own emotions.

"Dawn, come back here," Evan shouted as she ran up the stairs.

"Gary, you sit on that chair. You can play with the radio, but don't you dare come upstairs," Evan ordered in a voice that made even the agitated little boy pay attention.

At the foot of the stairs Evan stopped to warn him again.

"Now, be a good boy and stay in the basement. You're perfectly all right here, but be sure that you mind me."

Knowing that Evan would follow her, Dawn's first reaction was to get to her car, but she was too frightened of the tornado touching down to run all the way to the barn across open land. Trying to take refuge in her room, she was too slow, and Evan burst into the room before she could lock both doors.

"Are you crazy?" he yelled. "Get back downstairs!"

"Leave me alone," she said, demanding with her voice but pleading with her eyes.

The storm broke then, battering the house with tremendous force, turning the room an ominous green as the windows became watery portholes in their ark of survival.

He took her arm, intending to pull her toward the relative safety of the basement, but the emotional storm between them exploded, making his touch seem charged with electricity.

"Dawn," he said hoarsely, pulling her close.

His grip on her arms was brutally hard, and she fought him impulsively but without success. A horrendous roll of

138

thunder seemed to shake the room, but it didn't make her willing to find sanctuary in his arms.

"Let me go to the basement," she cried over the noise of the storm, grasping at this one chance of escaping him.

"It doesn't matter now," he said, his lips only inches from hers.

He kissed her, taking possession of her will, punishing her mouth while he delivered a silent message of longing. For a brief, intense moment he seemed to fill her consciousness as completely as he filled her vision, thrusting his hands under her shirt and pressing hard fingers against soft flesh.

"I hear Gary," Dawn said, straining her ears to catch the muffled call of the child over the roar of the storm.

"He's safe in the basement," Evan said impatiently.

"No, I hear him in the hall," she insisted, pushing at Evan to free herself.

"He's okay. Don't use him as an excuse."

"How can you say that! He's only a little boy and he's never seen a storm like this. I've got to go to him."

The sound Gary made was only a soft whimper, but now Evan heard it too. With an exasperated sigh, he released her and ordered her to stay where she was, moving toward the door himself and looking into the shadowy hall, unnaturally dimmed by the storm.

"Gary, I told you to stay in the basement," he said with a severity that infuriated Dawn. "When I say something, I mean it."

She protested vehemently, but her words fell on deaf ears. With a sudden but controlled motion, Evan turned Gary over and spanked him with quick, hard slaps.

Dawn could almost feel the stinging blows on her own bottom, and she cried out in protest.

"Evan! He's only a little boy afraid of a storm."

She raced toward the sobbing child, but Evan blocked her way, refusing to let her scoop him up and comfort him.

Furious because he was denying Gary the protection of her arms, she lashed out angrily at him.

"You didn't need to spank him!"

Evan's anger dissipated, but he didn't show a trace of remorse.

"His life could depend on his obedience," he argued, himself stung by the outrage on her face. "What happens if I tell him to stay away from the tractor, and he doesn't do it? Farm kids have to obey; their survival depends on it."

"He's only a little boy; you hit him because he interrupted you."

"I did not," he denied furiously. "He absolutely must learn to do as he's told."

"Maybe it won't be your job to teach him," she hissed angrily, longing to cradle the sobbing boy on her shoulder.

"You can be damn sure it won't be yours!"

The force of the storm outside subsided slightly, but Dawn felt as if she were caught in a tempest, tossed on a sea of longing and loathing, battered by waves of desire and righteous indignation. She wanted to hurt Evan because he had the means of causing her such anguish.

"Go away," she said furiously. "You've done your fatherly duty for today."

"Not without Gary," he said with dangerous calmness in his voice. "If I leave him to be coddled by your bleeding-heart foolishness, he won't understand why he was punished."

Letting him pick Gary up only because she couldn't have the child caught in a tug-of-war between the two of them, Dawn watched warily as he turned to Evan with no evident reluctance. In fact Gary stopped crying and seemed to regard the man with a mixture of curiosity and challenge.

She heard Evan's voice, calm and reasonable, explaining to Gary how important it was to obey, then the two of them went to check the weather warning on the radio.

"The tornado touched down just north of here, but didn't do much damage," he told her, coming to her door with Gary still in his arms. "Gary is going to play in his room now, and he won't come out until he has permission. Isn't that right, Gary?"

Gary didn't look enthusiastic, but he wasn't rebellious either. Dawn was impressed by Evan's follow-up of his punishment, but she couldn't forgive him for spanking Gary. If he thought he could park Gary in his room and come back to her, he was mistaken. It was sheer madness to think she could stay in Evan's house any longer, wanted but not loved, a second-rate baby-sitter with no real say in the terribly important job of raising Gary. She closed the door of her room and pushed in the lock on the knob, pacing anxiously, wondering if Evan would come back to her room, wanting him to do so only so she could reassert her feelings about how Gary should be treated.

She heard Evan's door close, and a few minutes later the shower added its splashing sound to the beating of the rain against the house. Remembering her first, and she hoped her only, cold shower, she wished Evan was suffering sufficiently to make up for the hard-handed spanking he gave Gary. With a flash of characteristic honesty, she knew she wanted him to suffer for his treatment of her too. What was happening between them had nothing to do with love or affection; they were engaged in the oldest war in history—one that women never won against their male opponents unless they remained cool, collected, and indifferent.

Evan hadn't held her in his home by force since the night he'd returned her keys, but he had used her feelings for him, raping her senses even when he avoided physical contact with her. He might be indifferent to her love, but he had to know that his nearness was a torment. The harder she tried to sort out her feelings for him, the more pain her love caused.

The shower stopped, and she fought against the vision of Evan emerging from the spray, his torso glistening, body hair curling damply against strong flesh. She didn't want to picture him in her imagination, drawing the towel vigorously across his shoulders, down to the small of his back, across his firm buttocks. She used gentle pats to dry herself, but she knew he must prefer rough swipes of the towel that stimulated his pores and left his untanned flesh glowing rosily. The thought of his coming to her still damp from the shower, his skin fragrant from spicy soap and tingling from his heavy-handed scrubbing, made her weak with desire. Because he was so alive and vibrant, the thought made her shiver, knowing her defenses against him weren't strong enough to withstand even a half-hearted attack.

It would never happen again, and she was a fool to be straining for sounds from behind the bathroom door. Evan Crane could drown in his shower, for all he meant in her life now. What had happened in the past between them must never come close to happening again. The time for an ultimatum had come.

Evan had Gary firmly under control, and he cared for him; she was sure of that. Whatever his birth records revealed, his future was secure. Evan wouldn't abandon him, even if Gary wasn't his son. Her strongest instincts told her that. There was no real reason for her to remain.

By the time she built up her courage to confront Evan, he was dressed and on his way out, wearing a rain slicker.

"I have to see what damage the storm did. If things are bad, I could be gone a long time," he told Dawn.

"I need to talk to you."

"It will have to wait," he snapped impatiently. "I have a lot of good neighbors. I've got to be sure no one needs help."

Someone does need help, she thought bitterly. She needed help in severing all ties with Evan Crane.

The rain never stopped completely that day, and the hours passed with torturing slowness. Several limbs were down in the yard, and the cornstalks in the nearby field had a tilted look from the battering they'd received, but there was nothing for her to do but wait out the tail end of the storm.

Gary was subdued, but not unhappy, and he was more interested than usual in the late afternoon lineup of children's shows on television. They ate dinner alone, and when Dawn went to bed close to midnight, Evan still hadn't returned.

CHAPTER EIGHT

Sometime in the night Evan returned and slept a few hours, but Dawn didn't hear him. Only a short note printed in his precise block letters indicated that he'd spent any time in the house. It read:

> Part of Clatts' barn collapsed. Family fine but animal casualties high. Don't expect me.
>
> E

Remembering Peter's pride in his prize-winning stock, Dawn immediately called Betty on the phone, offering any help she could give.

"Dewey and Evan and some other men are doing all that can be done," Betty said, trying to hide her dejection. "Peter's lost his best sow, Isabelle, for sure, and the vet isn't too optimistic about the little runt, Harvey. The horse is all right, thank heavens. That part of the barn held."

Betty appreciated her call, even though there really wasn't anything Dawn could do. The Clatt family freezer could feed an army of volunteer workers. Betty's biggest worry was her son, who'd made the young farmer's mistake of becoming attached to his livestock and was taking his losses pretty hard. His mother had her hands full with problems only she could handle.

Dawn felt useless and out of it, her burden being that she had too much time on her hands to think about Evan and her lost opportunity in California. As far as the job and apartment went, she felt only a listless irritation; it just didn't seem that important anymore whether she found a job on the West Coast, the East Coast, or anywhere else. She was afraid her work would be basically the same in any large urban area, and she couldn't seem to summon the vigor and enthusiasm she needed to begin a new job search. The resignation she felt about her profession didn't carry over into her relationship with Evan; here her thoughts were so confused and painful that she tried to put them out of her mind.

Dusk had deepened into total darkness before Evan finally returned to eat one of Mrs. Winsch's freezer meals warmed in the microwave. He was withdrawn without being hostile and answered Dawn's few questions with a minimum of words. There was a wall between them that made them behave like polite strangers, and neither of them had the will to try to break it down.

Working eighteen hours a day, Evan was much too exhausted to cope with the problem of Gary's care, Dawn grudgingly realized, putting off the time when she would give him her ultimatum to find someone else to care for the child. Being totally honest with herself, she admitted that it didn't matter now when she left. She was only going home to begin the dreary chore of hunting for a new job, and she was completely lacking the zest and zeal needed to be successful. She needed time to recoup and rebuild her enthusiasm. Meanwhile she let time slip by, preferring a state of inertia to the hassle of making decisions.

She took Gary to see the Clatts' damaged barn once the animal carnage had been cleared and found that much of the repair work had been done. Tears came to Betty's eyes when she told Dawn how much their neighbors, and especially Evan, had done to help them, even though this was a busy time for farmers. Peter had been greatly comforted by Evan's gift of a young sow, and the vet had done wonders in saving several other animals.

As impossible as it seemed, a week slipped by after the storm, and Dawn still felt suspended in a vacuum, going through the motions of living without really being in control. Only Gary's routine gave her a focus for each day, and she knew that, loving him as she did, leaving him was going to be dreadful. She knew, too, that she was following a cowardly course by letting her decision slide. Sooner or later she had to start rebuilding her life.

After days of Evan's silence and remoteness, she was totally unprepared for his Sunday afternoon project. He left the property in his pickup truck, then returned with Dewey and Peter following him in their truck. They unloaded piles of pipes and a sack of cement before the intent of all the activity became clear. Evan was installing a backyard play set for Gary, complete with slide, swings, and monkey bars.

When Gary learned the purpose of all their work, he was wild with excitement, and Dawn had her hands full keeping him out of the men's way. With three of them working, it still took the better part of the afternoon to dig holes, mix the cement, and assemble the many parts. Restraining Gary until the cement hardened was hard labor.

At Dawn's suggestion Evan invited Dewey and his son to stay for supper, and she called Betty and Tammy. Unused to fixing meals for large groups, she didn't say no when Betty offered to bring an apple-sauce cake fresh from the oven, but she did manage a respectable pot of spaghetti.

Dawn surprised herself by having fun. Some of her lethargy left her, and she felt a sense of accomplishment that she'd been able to return Betty's hospitality with some measure of success, even though cooking was low on her list of interests.

The climax of the evening came when the men decided it was all right for Gary to try out his slide. He accepted his good fortune with undiluted joy, but Dawn was more than a little puzzled by Evan's gift. The swing set was a permanent fixture, something meant to be used for years in the same place. What did it signify about Gary's future?

Social evenings ended early in Iowa; there was always the unrelenting work that another day would bring. Dawn found herself alone with Evan before she felt ready to confront him, but she didn't want him to retreat to his office or bedroom before she could talk to him.

Her question sounded more abrupt than she'd intended.

"Why did you put up the swing set for Gary?"

If he heard a note of accusation in her question, he ignored it.

"A kid needs outdoor activity."

"He does if he's staying. Are you admitting that he's your son?"

"Listen to yourself, Dawn. You make it sound like I'm on trial."

"You are, as a father!"

"Don't try to hang labels on me. I bought a toy so Gary can be outside without getting into trouble."

"That's all?"

"No, I suppose not," he said wearily. "If you want me to admit I feel a little guilty about punishing Gary, then I do. Let's leave it at that."

"That explains giving him a present, but why something that's cemented into the ground on your farm?"

"Drop it, Dawn," he said harshly, walking out of the room so she couldn't probe further.

She turned on the television, but an hour later she couldn't have said what had been on the screen. Her mind was too busy racing through a complicated maze, hitting detours and dead ends whichever way she explored. She knew, and had known in her heart for some time, that Evan wanted Gary to be his son, but did that mean the child was assured of a home, even if Sheila was his mother and an unknown man his father? If so, Dawn's reason for being in Evan's home was gone. She didn't know anymore how she felt about that, but leaving was going to be the most painful act of her life. Still, staying wasn't much better. Evan's aloofness was a constant torment, one she didn't think she deserved.

Her body cried out for rest, but her senses were totally awake, hearing the tiniest sounds of the night and imagining others. Even though the width of two large closets and a bathroom separated her room from Evan's, she was sure she heard him moving long after he'd gone to his room. She strained to hear more, frozen in a state of alertness, not wanting to rustle the sheets or breathe too heavily in case she missed some faint sound.

Evan's door opened; that was a noise she could hear clearly, and in a few moments he seemed to be in the kitchen. Lying motionless, she traced his late night prowlings with her ears, hearing the low but unmistakable sound of the TV.

How could a man who worked as hard as Evan fail to collapse and lose consciousness whenever he had a chance? She sat in the middle of the bed, drawing up her knees and resting her chin on them, wanting him to sleep so the dark shadows under his eyes would be erased.

No, she didn't want him to sleep, she admitted guiltily. She wanted him beside her, holding her, making love to her the way he had that dawn in the motel. That was why her eyes felt glued open and her mind was racing over a hundred unrelated thoughts.

Was that why Evan was roaming the house? How simple, then, to bring them both relief and rest. All she had to do was creep down the hallway, stand in the doorway to the family room, smile fetchingly, and drop her nightgown to the floor. What could be easier and more logical than to invite the man she loved into her bed?

What could be more impossible?

There wasn't a single reason for believing that Evan still

wanted her. He barely spoke to her anymore, and when he did, he was sullen and abrupt. If she threw away her pride and self-respect and tried to seduce him now, what could she hope to gain? Another brief interlude of love-making would be worse than nothing. Someday soon she was leaving, and that would be the end of everything.

At least she fell asleep before he returned to his room. It wasn't much satisfaction in the light of day, but it was something to know that his nights were disturbed too.

After a few cooler days, the relief brought by the rain-storm was over; temperatures soared, hitting the one hundred-degree mark two days in a row, and mugginess added to the discomfort. Attracted by his new play set, Gary couldn't get enough of being outdoors, but only the early hours of the morning were cool enough for him to be out in the sun. Evan spent more time than before working in his office, but his door was always shut, making it seem to Dawn that she spent all of her time alone with Gary. On the second day of the ferocious heat, the house ceased being a refuge from the savage weather; the overworked central air-conditioning stopped functioning. Even with every window and door open, the house seemed airless and as hot as an oven.

The firm that had installed the system some years before was swamped with work, and even when Evan cajoled a repairman into checking his unit, it looked like they'd be without cool air for some time.

"I'll call Des Moines and order the part right away," the harried technician said, "but this summer has been something else. Delivery time is running a week to ten days."

"What about calling the manufacturer direct?" Evan asked.

"I've tried it. It's quicker to get my order on the distributor's list in Des Moines. Sorry, I'll do the best I can."

Not taking one man's word, Evan spent a long time on

the phone, but he finally had to admit defeat. There was no way to hurry along the repair work.

"We'll just have to sweat, I guess," he said.

"If you say 'my grandfather did,' I'll scream," Dawn said, forcing a laugh to show him that the inconvenience wasn't all that important to her.

In fact she was slightly irritated by his concern. A little hot weather wasn't going to throw her into a tizzy, for goodness' sake. He must think she was a frail little hot-house flower.

The effect on their dispositions, not the heat itself, was the hard part. Gary developed a perpetual whine, or so it seemed to Dawn as she tried to keep him busy and happy. He had a heat rash, and no amount of tub time or powder seemed to help it. She called a doctor, but he didn't think he needed to see Gary; instead he telephoned a prescription for ointment to the nearest pharmacy. With the temperature still hitting the high nineties every day, it didn't work very well in clearing it up, but it did seem to give relief from the burning itch.

Because she had to restrain herself so often during the day to keep from yelling at Gary, who had a good reason for feeling cross, Evan was fair game when he did join her. He seemed to store up all his spleen for her too, and they snapped at each other over little things, sometimes letting bigger issues slip to the surface.

"Can't you see that Gary picks up his toys?" he asked after dinner one evening, pushing aside a plastic airplane with his foot.

"He does, at bedtime. You can't expect a three-year-old to be perfectly neat all the time."

"I expect him to learn a few elementary things, like not leaving things where they'll trip people."

"I look where I'm walking. You could do the same when there's a baby in the house."

"He's not a baby, and I don't expect my house to be an obstacle course."

"Then hire a full-time housekeeper!"

"Mrs. Winsch is enough."

"She hasn't been here all week."

"She always takes two weeks off in the summer. Do you begrudge her a vacation?"

"How fortunate that you have an unpaid replacement."

"I'll see that you're suitably reimbursed. I offered to pay you when you first came."

"Don't bother. I'm not Sheila, and I'm not for hire. If your incompetent lawyers and detectives would do their jobs, I'd be delighted to leave."

"I just bet you would!"

Almost every time they were in the same room, a quarrel sizzled under the surface, sometimes breaking out, but never really exploding into a full-scale fight. It was like letting steam escape just enough to keep a furiously boiling pot from spilling over. They managed to contain the emotional holocaust that was building between them, but Gary suffered from their hostile bickering. He threw his own tantrum during dinner one evening, knocking over his cup of milk and spraying it all over everything, and Evan packed him off to bed with no-nonsense firmness.

"It's our fault, you know," Dawn accused him, following Evan into his office, where he'd taken refuge, leaving the mess for her to clean up.

For a moment she thought he would argue, but he said with resignation, "I know it."

Dawn was surprised at herself because she felt real disappointment that Evan had sidestepped a quarrel. She needed to explode, to have all the tension between them brought out into the open, regardless of the high cost. Instead, she left his sweltering office with the door closed and went out to the patio to catch the faint breeze that was nudging the hot air masses ever so slightly.

"Iowa is too damn hot," she said aloud, but it wasn't the heat that was making her fidget.

She took Gary outside early the next morning, letting him swing, slide, and climb until he finally had his fill for a while. He was overheated, but calmer because of his vigorous play. His bath left her limp from the heat in the steamy bathroom, but after lunch it seemed that he would settle down peacefully for a nap. She needed one herself by that time.

Soaking in cool water was the most pleasurable thing she could think of doing, so she filled the tub for herself and gratefully stripped off her damp clothing. Lying with her head resting on the rim of the tub and enjoying her solitude, she nearly dozed.

"My God, why don't you lock the door?" Evan stood in the doorway that opened onto his room.

She sat upright and covered her breasts with her arms, trying to excuse her carelessness to herself more than to him.

"I forgot to check it after I gave Gary a bath, but you haven't been coming home for lunch. I thought I was alone in the house!"

"I did come home today, obviously."

Stark naked, he wrapped the towel he was carrying around his waist, but not before she saw the effect she'd had on him.

"I was hot," he said, trying to will himself to look away, to leave the room, but remaining nevertheless.

"So was I."

Knowing that she should tell him to leave, she sat motionless, noticing, quite beside the point, that her toes were puckered from her long soak.

"Are you cool now?" he asked in a voice filled with conflict.

"Yes, you can have the tub."

She wasn't surprised, nor did she protest, when he

dropped his towel to the floor and stepped into the water. Instead, she pulled up her knees to make room for him.

"Will you wash my back?" he asked hoarsely, picking up a large sponge shaped like a boat that Gary played with during his bath.

Nodding dumbly, Dawn spread her legs to make room for him, clutching at the damp sponge while he turned his back to her. Her legs slid against his hips and thighs, making her think that the current in the tub would electrocute them both, and she squeezed the tepid water over his shoulders, watching the rivulets stream down his back and disappear at the waterline.

"Scrub hard."

Saturating the surface of the sponge with soap, she attacked his lightly freckled, golden-brown back with hard, nervous swipes, washing away imaginary dirt until his skin glowed with pink undertones. Shuddering, his hand found her knee under the water and moved upward to caress her thigh.

He stood then, dripping water over her arms and breasts, towering over her, trembling ever so slightly.

"Don't do a halfway job," he pleaded, turning to guide her hand still holding the soapy sponge.

It was too much for Dawn. She stood and was stepping out of the tub when he caught her in his arms.

His kiss was possessive, claiming her mouth with a sureness that denied all the estrangement of the past days. When she pulled away and ran from him, he didn't try to stop her, but he did follow.

To find her bathrobe, she had to fumble through the clothing in her closet with shaking hands, managing to take a ridiculously long time to locate it and pull it on. Evan watched her from the other side of the room, not noticing that he was dripping on the light cream carpeting. He held a towel in one hand but didn't use it to dry or cover himself. His appraisal of her body was so frankly sensual that Dawn felt herself blushing.

"Why put on a robe?" he challenged.

"Evan, this is crazy. We've hardly been speaking for days. How can we get together now?"

"The same way we did before. Two bodies, blessedly different, one intent. It never seemed complicated before."

"It is complicated! I'm your baby-sitter, not your mistress."

"We've made it complicated, but it shouldn't be. I want you, and you want me, Dawn. Deny it, and I'll leave."

"You make it sound simple, but it isn't."

"Deny it."

"Evan, listen to me. I don't know what I want—"

"Tell me you don't want me, Dawn, if you can."

"Stop this!"

"I have stopped. I'm waiting."

"Please don't do this to me!"

"To you! Do you know how long it's been since I've had a good night's sleep? I ache for you, Dawn!"

"Evan!"

She was fighting with herself, not him. Why couldn't she say the simple words that would send him away? She believed he would go if she demanded it, but her love was confusing her senses and weakening her will.

Aggressiveness then would have frightened her into rejecting him, but he moved slowly, dropping his towel, walking toward her, and taking her shoulders in his hands as he looked into her face with undisguised longing.

"May I kiss you?"

She nodded, moistening her dry lips with the tip of her tongue before his mouth closed gently over hers. Deliberately, he kept his kisses on the surface, lightly brushing her lips with his until her tiny moan made him bolder.

The room was a hot box, with the single window failing to catch the slightest movement of air. He found a sensitive spot in the hollow of her neck, and spasms of pleasure made her tremble.

Ripping free the belt of her robe, he let it fall open and stepped closer to press his heated flesh against hers.

"No!" she cried out with a vehemence that made him back away instinctively.

"I said I'd leave if you wanted me to," he choked out, his disappointment hanging between them like a leaden shield.

Dawn turned her face away in confusion, loving and wanting him with every atom of her being, but determined not to fall into the same pattern again. There was nothing she wanted more at that moment than to make love with him, but it wouldn't change anything. Afterward she would still be a hanger-on in his household, unsure of his feelings for her, and unready to plan any kind of a future for herself. Because she did love him painfully and wholly, she had to deny them both the bliss of immediate fulfillment.

"I'll go," he said so dejectedly that she was driven to pull herself together.

"No, I don't want you to leave," she said.

The urgency in her voice gave him new hope, and he waited, motionless and silent, for her to say more.

"Could you put something on?" she begged, needing to eliminate the distraction of his nakedness.

He bent and retrieved his bath towel, wrapping it around his waist without taking his eyes from her.

Sitting stiffly on the edge of the bed, she groped for a way to tell him how she felt. A confession that she loved him too much to make love to him just for the pleasure it brought them seemed impossible to put into words. If he didn't really care for her, then his touch was torture, and she wanted to be released from the prison love had made for her, first her love for Gary, then her reckless, totally consuming love for Evan. Because she had too much to say, all words seemed to evade her.

Sitting beside her without touching her, he seemed to sense her dilemma and tried to begin for her.

"We need to talk, don't we?"

"Yes," she barely whispered, grateful for any flicker of understanding from him.

"There's more to this than just going to bed together," he said thoughtfully. "I should have realized a lot of things, but I'm stubborn, Dawn, and used to getting my own way."

"I don't want an apology, Evan."

"I'm not apologizing. You're the first woman I've cared for since . . ." He stopped without finishing his thought.

"Since your wife left you? Say it, Evan, say what you're thinking. Otherwise nothing can happen between us ever again."

"That sounds like blackmail, Dawn. If I don't let you probe my mind, I can't have you."

"That's crude, and you know it."

"Yes, I do. I will apologize for that, but you can't put me under a microscope and build a case history out of my foibles and follies."

"I'm not like that!" she protested, hurt by his attitude. "Dawn."

The little voice was near them, much nearer than Gary's room, and Evan hurried to the closed door, opening it enough to see the little boy standing outside.

"Hey, Gary, naptime isn't over. You go right back to your room. You can play with your toys if you're not sleepy, but don't come out until I tell you it's time."

After seeing that Gary went into his room, Evan closed the door softly and walked to the bed, where Dawn was sitting. His toes sank into the pile of the rug, and Dawn kept her eyes riveted on his ankles and the firmness of his calves, not daring to raise her eyes to meet his. Now that they were really going to talk, she felt tongue-tied and timid, and he wasn't going to say anything that would make it easier for her, she feared.

"Dawn."

He sat and took her hand, but she pulled it away as if his fingers burned her. Her resolve was too flimsy to risk his touch. She needed something from him, and without it her future stretched ahead with unrelieved bleakness.

"No touching?" he asked, forcing a light tone into his voice.

She shook her head.

"Where do we start?" he asked.

"At the beginning."

"When I wouldn't let you leave?"

"Yes."

"I didn't want you to leave me. It had nothing to do with Gary."

"And now?"

"I still don't. More than ever."

"You didn't shave this morning," she said, changing the subject as a defensive action but hating herself for being a coward. What she needed to hear had to come from Evan without her prompting, and she didn't know just how to talk to him.

"I didn't, did I?" He took one of her hands and rubbed it against his beard, then, remembering that she didn't want to be touched, he dropped it abruptly.

"Making love to you has been the main thing on my mind since the first moment I saw you," he said solemnly.

Daring to look at him, she saw new lines of fatigue radiating from his eyes and realized that the situation between them had been as hard on him as it had been on her. She wanted to cradle his head against her breast and soothe away his weariness, but it was too soon.

"Then why have we been so far apart, Evan?"

He couldn't stop himself from taking her hand in his,

bringing it to his lips, kissing it softly, then pressing it against his cheek again. She couldn't bring herself to protest.

Words seemed superfluous, and the heat in the room was insignificant compared to the raging furnace of their emotions. Dawn felt a tidal wave welling up inside her, but this time her whole life seemed to hang in the balance; she moved away quickly, standing to evade Evan's compelling touch.

"I'm not good at following rules I don't make," he admitted with a boyish grin.

"No, you're not," she agreed.

"Are you really going to leave me?" he asked in a voice made husky with yearning.

Now it seemed urgent that there be nothing but the truth between them. She took a deep breath and answered.

"The job in California is taken."

"I made you lose it, but it's hard to say I'm sorry."

"There's more. The apartment is gone too. Maggie's fiancé is moving in with her."

"Oh." His single word hung heavily in the air, then he added, "You have good reason to hate me."

"I don't."

"I hope not. I've never wanted anyone more in my life. Sit by me again."

She moved slowly, her love battling with her common sense and winning. As she sat down an accidental glance at her bedside clock made her suddenly apprehensive. Ordinarily Gary's naptime would be over. He was being too good, and for him, that often meant trouble. She was sure he hadn't called her since Evan had sent him back to his room. Living with him had given her a mother's sensitivity to his call.

"I'd better check on Gary. He's been awfully patient."

"The heat probably knocked him out, but you're right. We'd better check on him, but I'm not going back to work.

Not until we understand each other perfectly. We have a lot more to talk about."

Gary's door was closed, so Dawn breathed a little easier. All the outdoor play in the heat that morning must have exhausted him. Still, her instinct told her to look in on him, even if it meant waking him.

The room was empty, his bed rumpled but not occupied.

"Gary!" she called loudly outside his door, bringing Evan to her.

"Where is he?" he asked.

"I don't know. Not in his room. Gary, don't play games!" she yelled even louder.

"Little rascal," Evan said, not sounding alarmed. "I've told him enough times not to leave his room after naptime without permission."

"Help me look," Dawn said.

Evan took a few moments to run into his room and hurriedly dress, then he joined her in her search.

A glance into the family room did not bring the sight they had wished for. Gary couldn't open the sliding glass door because of its heaviness, but today this door had been left open to admit more air, and only the light screen had been closed. Now it was open a foot or so, just enough for one little boy to slip outside.

"My God!" Evan said for both of them. "He's gone off on his own."

CHAPTER NINE

Standing behind Evan, Dawn didn't have a clear view of the backyard, and her first thought was that Gary must have gone outside to play on his swing set.

"He's on the swing, isn't he?" she asked.

"No, see for yourself."

With Evan she went through the patio door out into the full force of the afternoon sun to stand, frowning, in the bright light.

"Apparently he's wandered off," Evan said, trying to conceal the anxiety he was feeling.

"He wouldn't go far, he just wouldn't. He loves hide-and-seek, Evan. It's his favorite game. He's just hiding somewhere so we'll chase after him. Look under the spruce branches. He's probably there."

"Maybe. Check the house just to be sure he isn't inside. Don't overlook anyplace where he could be hiding—under beds, behind furniture, in closets. You'd better check the freezer in the basement too."

"I don't think he can open it."

"Check anyway," he said more harshly than he intended; then he quickly apologized for snapping at her.

Dawn got the message; he was worried, and that made her even more anxious.

"I'll check everywhere," she assured him.

"I'll go through the barn, check the truck and tractors. There are so damn many places a little kid could hide."

She watched Evan for a brief moment as he ran across

the yard, stopping to stoop under the branches of a massive evergreen and calling Gary's name loudly. Trying to ignore the knot of apprehension in her midsection, she began to search on the patio, looking behind the glider, the only possible place of concealment in the screened area.

Deciding that a quiet search was best, she quickly but thoroughly looked through the main floor room by room. If Gary was playing a game, her calls would give him a warning of her presence. The last bedroom she searched was hers, and the sight of the bed made guilt well up like bile in her throat. Gary wouldn't have crept off on his own if she and Evan hadn't been so lost in each other. A foolish compulsion made her take a moment to smooth the bedspread where they had sat, as though by erasing the evidence that they'd been there wrapped up in each other she could block out the consequences.

The house was ominously quiet, and even though the basement was a little cooler than the upstairs, Dawn felt as though she was struggling through a steam room. Drenched with perspiration, she was also parched, her throat aching with nervous dryness.

It didn't take long to exhaust all the possibilities. She even checked the round, watery pit that housed the sump pump, thrusting in a broom handle to see how deep it was. It was much too shallow to conceal the body of a child Gary's size. The pantry storage room, the furnace area, Evan's workshop—all were empty. She even checked the huge chest freezer as Evan had suggested. Gary simply was not in the house. If he had been, he wouldn't have been able to resist the chance to pop out and "boo" her.

Evan's search of the barn and utility area had taken as long as her examination of the house, and she met him outside, looking into the interior of her car through the windows. He even got down on his knees and looked under it.

"No luck?" he asked needlessly.

"No. Evan, he wouldn't wander into the fields after all your warnings. He just wouldn't!"

"We have to believe that he did. He isn't anyplace else."

"Maybe Sheila came and took him. She threatened it."

"Dawn, we don't have time to grasp at straws. Sheila doesn't want Gary, and she didn't take him."

"You can't be sure."

"I can. I paid her," he said wearily.

In her anxiety over Gary, Dawn didn't have time for the shock to register. She pushed all her questions, and she had many, to the back of her mind to concentrate on the only one that really counted.

"What should we do?"

"Let's gamble that he hasn't gotten far. You start at the corner of that field, and I'll do the same. We'll work our way in opposite directions until we go full circle and meet again. Stop and call as loudly as you can every few feet."

"The corn is so thick, we wouldn't see him if he was there," she said anxiously.

"He'll want to be found. Just let him hear your voice, and he'll answer."

"Evan, I'm scared."

"So am I."

They both ran, Evan moving easily over the rough perimeter of the fields bordering the cleared area and the house, Dawn stumbling several times as she tried to hurry in sandals that were more decorative than practical. Perspiration ran from her forehead, clouding her eyesight, and the direct rays of the sun made her feel light-headed. It seemed to take forever to make the circle, and her throat burned from calling every few feet in an increasingly frantic voice.

When Evan loomed ahead of her, she ran toward him, collapsing in his arms.

"I didn't hear a thing," she said brokenly. "Oh, Evan, where is he?"

"We're going to need help, that's for sure. Listen, I'll check the barn once more, just to be sure he didn't double back on us, and you call the Clatts. Tell Betty Gary may be lost in the fields, and we need help. She'll start a telephone chain."

"Yes, I'll do that."

"And, honey, don't come back out without a hat." He touched her deeply flushed cheek with the back of his hand.

"I am woozy. Oh, no! Gary left his cowboy hat on the dresser. He's out there in the heat with only his shorts and T-shirt. He's so little, Evan."

"Call the Clatts," he said, his voice stern from the effort of masking his anxiety.

Betty didn't waste time trying to reassure Dawn with useless platitudes. She hung up immediately to begin summoning neighbors who would drop everything to join the search.

Feeling her own limitations acutely, Dawn went into the bedroom and changed from her shorts and skimpy top to more protective jeans and a long-sleeved cotton blouse. Her shoulders and the backs of her knees were stinging from exposure to the sun, and it was terrifying to think what the sun would do to Gary's fair skin. She could only hope the tall stalks would give him some shelter.

Her tennis shoes would help her move through the fields more easily too, and in the coat closet she found a battered straw hat that once had been a lady's rather elegant lawn hat. She plopped it on her head without even wondering if it had been Evan's mother's or his wife's. He was hatless too, she remembered, grabbing a western-style straw from the top shelf for him.

She found him at the edge of a field, his voice hoarse from continued calling. He put on the hat without comment, his face frowning with anxiety.

"It's bad, isn't it?" she asked needlessly. "Like the little boy you told me about. But Gary doesn't have three days, does he? Evan, it's so hot. He'll dehydrate. We've got to find him."

"We have to—yes."

Even in her own misery, she saw the tears clouding his eyes and realized how much this child meant to him.

"If only we hadn't left him alone so long," she began.

"It was my fault," he said. "I knew Gary couldn't be trusted on his own for very long. There just hasn't been enough time to teach him everything he needs to know to survive on a farm. He should have been my first priority."

Not you lay unspoken between them, but even unsaid, the thought stabbed Dawn.

"I made him my responsibility by bringing him here, and I failed him," she admitted.

"Standing here feeling sorry for ourselves won't find him." He walked away, hoarsely calling "Gary."

Dewey and his two children arrived first, but other neighbors followed as quickly as the distance of their farms allowed. For a while people of all ages seemed to mill around aimlessly, but the pattern of their search soon became clear under Evan's clear-headed direction. Masking his own fears, he assigned areas and suggested a search strategy to each individual, while Dawn watched, feeling useless.

"Where should I search, Evan?" she asked him when she had a chance.

"Nowhere."

"I have to."

"Honey, your face is redder than a tomato. You won't help by passing out. Go into the barn and find the gallon thermos jugs in the closet over by the south wall. Fill them with water, and I'll have people carry them out to the fields. We can't have anyone getting sick on us, and the main cause is dehydration."

"I could make some lemonade too."

"Do it, but fill all the water jugs first."

She wanted to be in the thick of the search, giving her last ounce of strength to find Gary, but Evan's practical orders made more sense. When Betty came to help her with the water, the job seemed more important.

"The little scamp," Betty said, dealing with her fears by fretting. "Whatever got into him to slip away from you like that? Evan said he was supposed to be napping. You have the makings of a good cat burglar there, the way he got out on you."

Betty's words were like a rawhide lash on Dawn's conscience. It hadn't been hard for Gary to leave the house on his own. He could have made enough noise for a motorcycle caravan, she thought, and they wouldn't have heard him, involved as they were with each other. In her mind she could see the two of them sitting together on the bed while Gary opened his door, closed it behind him, and walked out of the house in search of entertainment. She'd heard every sound the night when Evan had moved restlessly through the house, kept awake by his longing for her, but she'd been deaf to the little boy whose care had kept her there.

Misinterpreting the look of total dismay on Dawn's face, Betty stopped talking and took her in her arms.

"They'll find him," she promised her. "Gary's bright enough to answer if he hears them."

Dawn shook her head dumbly, trying not to give way to tears. She didn't deserve sympathy. If Betty knew the truth, she'd be appalled at her irresponsibility.

Ignoring Evan's orders and Betty's pleas, Dawn felt compelled to go back to the fields, the compulsion to be close to the search strengthened by the gnawing feeling that she'd somehow failed Gary. She saw Evan emerging from a row of corn that topped his head and raced toward him.

"Nothing," he said, anticipating her question.

165

For a brief instant they held each other, but there wasn't any comfort for them in each other's arms. She didn't need to talk to him to know that his conscience was torturing him even more acutely than hers, if that was possible. It was a measure of her love that she felt compassion, not blame, for his share in their carelessness. She felt the full burden should be hers.

"We've got to get the sheriff in on this," he said. "I'm going in to call now."

"So many people are here."

"Not nearly enough to cover the fields we have to search. The trouble is, he can wander so far without coming out on a road or to another house. There's nothing but corn for acres and acres. Oh, damn it all, how could I let this happen?"

"It was my fault. I should have postponed our talk."

"Don't be silly. I wouldn't have gone. I've been feeling like a bull in rut, and I couldn't face another night without some understanding between us."

"Evan, don't!" She hurried beside him toward the house.

"Don't what?"

"Don't be so hard on yourself. Let me shoulder some of the blame. I am anyway."

"We don't have time to talk about this," he said dejectedly.

She followed him into his office, where he went to use the phone, even though it was a waste of her time to be with him. His voice was calm and businesslike as he talked to the sheriff. The law officer, Dawn remembered, was a high school friend and teammate of Evan's. There was something comforting about being able to call on old friends in a time of crisis, she decided. Without the prop of familiar faces from her past, she felt her aloneness very keenly. She needed something from Evan, a hint of encouragement, a pat of affection, a word of absolution—all things his anxious emotional state wouldn't allow him to give.

When he hung up the phone, she saw real suffering in his eyes, but he quickly averted his face, too filled with self-loathing to accept her pity. Having his friends and neighbors heap their sympathy and help on him only added to his discomfort, Dawn knew. She could help him best by pretending to be confident and optimistic, conditions she didn't feel.

"What did the sheriff say?" she asked.

"He'll alert the radio station to ask for more help and come himself with all the deputies he can spare. He wants to try using dogs right away. The trouble is, it's so damn hot. We have to find him quickly."

"What do you want me to do?" she asked, knowing that giving orders and planning were the things that helped him keep his control.

As miserable as she felt, she sensed that his pain was even deeper. There wasn't time to question why, but the knowledge of his suffering was locked into her mind, something she would have to examine and discuss with him when Gary was found. When, not if! He simply had to be found and found soon. A bright, alert boy, he would try to get back to them. He just couldn't miss all the activity of the search party.

What had Evan or Betty told her about the little boy lost for three days? The searchers must have passed close by, but he was frightened and hid. Gary wouldn't do that; he wasn't afraid of people. He would go to the searchers unless he panicked, unless he was unconscious already. *Unless!* A terrible word!

"If the search lasts long, we'll have to feed people," Evan said. "Talk to Betty and see what she thinks should be done."

Betty was a wonderful organizer, Dawn knew, but suddenly she didn't want to hand over this responsibility to her. It was time she took charge herself.

"I'll handle it," she told Evan. "Having a restaurant bring in food is the only practical way. How many people are here?"

"I'm not sure. We can expect hundreds more with the radio appeal for help."

Much as she wanted to follow him back to the fields, she stayed inside and found that the house had become a hub of activity, a virtual command post for the search. The radio brought in volunteers from all over the county, and some people brought food with them, possibly their own dinners they'd started to prepare, leaving it in the kitchen in anticipation of long hours of work. People Dawn had never seen before gave her their support, prayers, and food, and sometimes she had to choke out her thanks, so deeply touched was she by the response.

Betty had commandeered a few of the older women who should not be walking the fields in such heat, and they were organizing a massive outdoor spread of food, hopefully as a reward for success, but possibly just to keep people going. Dawn told them her idea of calling a restaurant for help and made the contact herself, explaining the problem and what they needed. The owner of a modest family restaurant agreed to fry chicken and bring ham and rolls to supplement the donations they were still receiving, and arranged to bring it the twelve miles or so to the farm in his van as soon as possible.

The heat was building inside the house and outside, with no breeze for relief, and Dawn had terrible visions of Gary literally frying to death under the merciless rays of the late afternoon sun. Fortunately she was kept too busy to dwell on her worst fears, since the house was a frantic center of activity. The sheriff's men arrived, and the dog handler sought her out to get some objects Gary had used recently. He was a gangling adolescent with big feet and hands, his face still dotted with pimples. To Dawn he looked much too young to be a deputy sheriff, and she would have been happier with a gray-bearded veteran with lots of experience. She did realize she was being unfair to the young man; he might know his job very well. Certainly he seemed confident.

Taking a moment to watch the specially trained hounds begin their work, she was encouraged when they seemed to be interested in one particular direction. Later she learned that they had found Gary's scent leading toward a south field, but he had had time for a lot of aimless wandering since entering the field at that spot.

"So many people are looking," she said to Betty during a particularly bleak moment when her fear surfaced. "Why can't they find him?"

Seeing that the look on Betty's face reflected her own desperation, she dug her nails into the palms of her hands, knowing she shouldn't try to lean on her friend.

"Scratch that," Dawn said. "I know how hard everyone's trying, and I know they'll find him."

"That's the way to talk," Betty said.

New searchers kept coming, and the lawn in front and back of the house looked like a parking lot. Dawn made the decision to open all the doors of the barn and set up food in there. It meant more work for the women, carrying everything out there, but it was closer to the fields and would waste less of the searchers' time. Planks and sawhorses were converted to tables, supplementing all those Dawn could find in the house. Besides the catered food and the donations, many easily thawed foods were taken from Evan's freezer by Dawn, so it looked like they had enough for everyone who wanted to eat.

Heat and discouragement had left their mark on the people who'd been tramping through the fields, but most of them ate a hasty meal and went back to cover new territory and look again through fields already searched.

They were red-faced, weary, dirty, and rank with perspiration; most were total strangers, but Dawn loved them all so much, she could hardly speak.

How long had it been since she'd seen Evan? Her heart ached for him, and she had to see how he was holding up. When he didn't come in to eat, she wrapped some chicken and rolls in foil and went looking for him, learning that he'd gone in a car with some men to try working the south field from the other extreme. There was no way she could deliver his dinner, but that didn't stop her from adding concern for him to her crushing anxiety over Gary.

The hours of summer daylight were still long, but the approaching dusk seemed to hurry toward them menacingly. Combing row by row of towering corn, unable to see each other and barely able to pass between the close lines of growth, the searchers were helpless when it came to hurrying the hunt. Using dangerous machinery was out of the question, and the drudgery of searching every row, the base of every stalk, seemed maddeningly slow.

Some people left, regretfully, because they had stock to feed or other urgent matters to attend, but no one left just because the search was hard and discouraging. Dawn was trembling with fatigue and anxiety, feeling useless now that the huge impromptu picnic had been served. She had to be with Evan.

The sun had dipped below the horizon, and there was only enough light left to distinguish people at close range, when she spotted him emerging from a field. Running toward Evan with energy drawn from some unsuspected source, she fell into his arms, pressing against him to receive and give comfort.

"Nothing," he said, pressing his face into her hair.

His body was shaking, and she realized that he was fighting not to break down.

They sat side by side on the ground beside the field, secluded by the near darkness and the black stalks towering nearby, not touching but drawing strength from each other.

"Sorry," Evan said hoarsely, wiping his face on a wadded handkerchief. "I just can't believe this is happening."

"We'll find him," Dawn said, willing herself to believe it, so he would.

"How? It's nearly dark. We couldn't find an elephant in there at night."

The despair in his voice shook her to the marrow, and she reached for his hand, pressing her head against it, trying to find some cause for optimism.

He rose slowly and pulled her up with him, holding her against him for a soul-sharing instant.

"We will find him," he said at last, sounding stronger and more like himself. "I'll get out all the lanterns and flashlights I have, and most of these people will have one or more lights in their cars or trucks. Maybe having it dark will help. Gary will be able to see lights, and if we get near him, he'll hear us."

She didn't believe him; the corn would block the lights just as it deadened the sound, but just hearing that he wasn't giving up made her false optimism seem real.

She insisted on going with Evan when he entered the north field, one that searchers had largely deserted now, hoping that the bloodhounds had been right in finding his scent going in the opposite direction.

"There's no way of guessing which way he wandered. He could have entered the south field and circled until he was in the opposite field," Evan said, explaining his choice. "I even get confused when I'm in the middle of a field. I have to check out the position of the sun."

A cornfield at night was a frightening place to Dawn. The visibility was nil, and the stalks seemed to press against her on all sides. Even with Evan beside her, his light in his hand, she was scared, imagining how terrified

171

Gary must be, alone, lost, tortured by thirst and hunger, maybe badly hurt.

"Are there any animals that will hurt him?" she asked faintly. "Snakes?"

"The snakes around here are mostly bull snakes. They're not poisonous. Now that the sun's gone, the mosquitoes and bugs are a bigger worry. You don't need to worry about animals, though, unless he's come across a skunk. There's been a rabies epidemic in them this year."

"Oh, God, help us to find him," she said fervently, wishing she hadn't asked about animals.

Mosquitoes were already attacking her. The walking was terrible too. She stumbled frequently, hurting her ankle but not so badly that she was willing to let Evan go on searching without her.

Moving slowly, Evan played his light on either side, and they took turns calling Gary's name. His physical resources were greater than hers, and she felt that she was slowing him down. Running to keep close to him, she took a headlong tumble, landing on her hands and knees on the dry, rough dirt. Before she could pull herself up, she heard a soft, muted sound close to the ground.

Straining her ears, she listened intently, sure that what she had heard hadn't been an animal or insect sound.

"Dawn, are you all right?" Evan asked, letting his light fall on her.

"Quiet," she warned urgently, leaning closer to the ground, trying to pick up the sound again.

Only silence rewarded her effort, but she was sure she hadn't imagined the faint whimper.

"I know I heard something, just a weak little sound, but something."

"Call as loudly as you can, then listen again," he ordered.

She called Gary's name so loudly, it seemed to hang there in the humid blackness of the night. Her forehead beaded with droplets as she bent forward rigidly on her hands and knees, praying that she'd hear the little sound again. When she did, it was still distant and indistinct, but it definitely wasn't her imagination.

"I heard it too," Evan said excitedly. "Gary! We're coming, Gary! Talk to us, Gary."

"Stay here and listen," he said. "I think it came from that direction." He dashed off through close-packed stalks, not caring if he bent or damaged them.

She didn't want to be left alone, but the possibility that they'd heard Gary made her willing to endure anything.

Evan moved in spurts, knocking aside corn and forcing his way forward, then pausing to listen for the slightest telltale sound. Hearing his movement, Dawn tried to determine if the noise he was making came from the same direction as the faint cries she'd heard.

"More to the right, Evan," she called out without being able to see him. "I heard it again."

"Dawn, come here!"

She ran, pushing through several rows, getting slapped in the face by vegetation, struggling to stay on her feet.

"I have him," Evan said, his words the most welcome she had ever heard.

"Gary, darling, are you all right?" she cried, half laughing and half crying in relief.

Evan picked him up gently and cushioned him against his chest, handing Dawn the flashlight.

"He's barely conscious, and he's been vomiting," he said urgently.

"What does that mean?"

"Heat stroke. We've got to get him to a hospital."

"Will he be all right?"

"I hope so."

He was already moving back the way they'd come, leaving Dawn to trail him with the flashlight. Hardly able to keep her own footing with the light to help her, she didn't know how Evan could carry Gary and run so surefootedly; the need to hurry must have given him some special grace.

Before they reached the barn, where Evan's powerful car was parked, the news had spread, bringing swarms of people to see for themselves that the missing child was all right.

"I'll never forget all of you," Evan said to the crowd after he'd handed Gary to Dawn, sitting in the car. "No one ever had better neighbors."

"You didn't need us, Evan," an older farmer joked. "Went and done the finding yourself." His humor reflected the relief they all felt.

"I needed you, all of you," he said fervently, ducking into the car.

Dawn couldn't remember the details of their race through the countryside, but she never forgot the sense of urgency and the growing dread that perhaps they had found him too late. The child was limp, listless, and damp, and even in the dark Dawn could tell there were nasty bumps and dried blood where his skin was exposed. All his injuries seemed to be small scratches and bug bites, but she wouldn't breathe easily until a doctor had thoroughly examined him.

The drive wasn't very long, only about thirty minutes, but it seemed to take forever. They carried him into an emergency room prepared for their coming by someone back at the farm, and a doctor was waiting to treat Gary.

The preliminary examination didn't seem to alarm the doctor, but he ordered Gary admitted to the hospital to be treated for heat stroke and for observation. He shook his head while they related the story of the search, some of which the doctor had already heard on the radio.

"Just wandered off on his own?" the physician asked,

the look of piercing perceptiveness on his face rather upsetting.

"That's right," Evan said, but Dawn could sense his tension as he stood beside her.

There would be others who asked questions. Why would a three-year-old boy be unwatched long enough to disappear in a cornfield? Even those who knew he wasn't a neglected child would shake their heads and say "You got to watch the little ones on a farm."

They went together to Gary's room to see him settled into the crib in the pediatric ward. Bathed and dressed in hospital pajamas with bears and balloons printed on them, he still looked terrible, his face a mass of swollen red lumps and scratches. His little hands tore at Dawn's conscience, covered as they were with nasty bites and abrasions, and the remorse she felt burrowed its way even deeper into her consciousness. She loved Gary, and she had let him down.

The doctor came into the room one more time after Gary had fallen asleep, taking pity on the adults' haggard, soiled appearance.

"There's nothing more you can do tonight," he assured them. "He may sleep all night now, and we watch the patients pretty closely on this floor. You might as well go home."

"When can we take him home?"

"We'll see in the morning. There's still his dehydration, and he's going to be uncomfortable for a while, but he should be fine in a few days."

"Thank God!" Evan said for both of them.

Never had Dawn felt so totally drained; she barely managed to put one foot in front of the other on the way out to the lot where Evan had parked the car. They walked side by side, not touching, and Dawn didn't need to see his face to know that the same self-anger she felt was eating away at him.

175

"Little boys do things like this," she said, wanting to comfort him even more than she wanted to punish herself.

"That's why they have to be watched, taught, even disciplined."

"You think I was too lenient," she said, remembering how she disagreed when Evan was firm in correcting Gary.

"No, he was never your responsibility."

"I made him mine."

"What choice did you have? I know enough about Sheila to realize that she maneuvered you into this."

"But you paid her, Evan. Why?"

"I don't feel like talking about it now, if you don't mind."

She did mind, but she understood too. If all they felt was physical exhaustion, conversation would have been possible. As it was, they both needed time to heal, to come to terms with their remorse.

They rode in total silence, relieved when they got back to the house that the yard was deserted, not one car or truck remaining of the fleet parked there by the hundreds of searchers. Their neighbors' final kindness of the day had been to leave them alone to drop exhausted into bed. Knowing that Betty, especially, would still be worrying, Dawn made a quick call to tell her the doctor's optimistic news. As she'd expected, both of the Clatts had found it impossible to get to sleep until they heard that Gary was all right.

"Thank you for calling," Evan said from where he had stood watching her use the phone.

He went into his room, closing the door with a soft bang that had a note of finality about it. She didn't hear a sound from his room, and she envied him if he had dropped into an exhausted sleep. She felt filthy and haggard and tired beyond belief, but she couldn't go to bed without washing off the dirt that peppered her skin. Too tired to really scrub, she just stood under a warm shower until her hair was soaked and her body cleansed of dirt and perspiration. If only she could wash clean her conscience as easily.

CHAPTER TEN

Barely awake, Dawn tried to brush away the source of the tickling beside her eye, but she struck a very solid, very alive object. Evan's face was so close to hers that she could feel the caress of his breath and the delicious prickliness of his early morning beard. Then, before she could move, he kissed her squarely on her mouth, bringing her fully awake with a cascade of sensations.

"Are you going to take advantage of me?" she mumbled.

"Not the way you're suggesting," he said with a small laugh. "I like my women awake and kicking."

"I can't kick. You're crushing my legs." It wasn't a rebuke.

"I'm leaving now, but I won't be gone long. As soon as I've talked to Dewey about a few things, I'll come back here, and we'll go to the hospital."

"Maybe I should call now," she said, pulling herself up on her elbow.

"I already have. It's too early for the doctor to be in, but the nurse on duty said Gary had a good night and is still sleeping."

"Evan, I still feel so guilty for leaving him alone too long."

"You shouldn't. It was my fault."

"No."

"It's just something we have to live with, but Gary is all right. That's what's important."

The serious, drawn look on his face told her that he couldn't dismiss his own remorse so easily, and she stroked his cheek softly to try to erase that feeling.

"There's one thing I have to ask you," he said with deep seriousness.

Dawn tensed, knowing that things between them had come to a head and would never be quite the same again.

"Wait until I'm awake," she said, trying to make light of their situation.

"I don't want an answer now. I just want you to think about marrying me."

"Oh," she gasped weakly.

"Will you marry me, Dawn? No, don't answer now." He laid two fingers gently over her lips.

"Don't you want to hear my answer?"

"Desperately, but not until you're wide awake and we've talked about some other things."

He stood beside the bed, a sad but sweet smile on his face that made her throat swell with tenderness. Her emotions told her to say yes immediately, but just knowing that he wanted her was enough for the moment.

Dressed only in a pair of faded jeans slung low on his hips, he sat beside her, pulling her into his arms, her nostrils filling with the dry, sun-baked scent of his skin. His kiss was sweetness and longing and promise, masking a desire so compelling that Dawn didn't know how she could endure a separation even of moments. Her heart gave her the only possible answer to his question, but she was willing to postpone the instant of acceptance because he wanted it that way.

After he left, she went through her morning routine in a rosy haze, not even noticing what she ate for breakfast. To know that there was nothing in the world she wanted more than to be Evan's wife was like coming home after a long and hazardous trip. The rightness of it was deeply satisfying.

She dressed to suit her fanciful mood in a flared cotton skirt and sleeveless blouse. The only shoes she had to match the emerald and blue hues of the skirt's design were some little slippers that she'd bought a long time ago at a shoe outlet because they reminded her of the ballet lessons she took as a child. A foolish purchase, she'd decided after buying them, but now they were a way of dressing up to be a new person. And she did feel new and fresh and glorious.

Something bad had happened to Gary, but he was all right now. She loved him and she loved Evan, and the horror of nearly losing the child had made her realize that she didn't want to lose his father either.

The thought of Evan as Gary's parent sobered her; how much longer would they be at loose ends, not knowing for sure about his birth? She'd believed in their blood relationship from the beginning, and Evan's distress yesterday made her sure he loved Gary as a son, with or without proof. Still, before she accepted his proposal, they should talk about it. There were unresolved questions, not the least of which was why he had paid Sheila.

On the drive to the hospital they avoided speaking about serious subjects; by unspoken agreement they needed time to feel the release of tension after yesterday's harrowing search. What they did marvel at and discuss was the instant and wholehearted response of friends, neighbors, and even strangers.

"Evan, they were just great! I couldn't believe it when I saw the cars and trucks and people."

"We'll never be able to thank them enough," he said.

"I think they had their thanks when we found Gary alive. People here just seem to care so much."

He smiled at her earnestness and squeezed her hand, bringing it to rest on his thigh.

The drive seemed much shorter than it had the night

before, and they reached the hospital before the official visiting hours began.

"Parents are exempt," Evan assured her as they bypassed the visitors' desk and went up in the elevator.

"Are you officially declaring yourself a parent?" she challenged.

"We'll talk about that and some other things after we check on Gary," he said.

They found Gary in the playroom, engrossed in a game with a candy-striper. Although he seemed glad to see them, he did insist on finishing the game, throwing plastic pieces in a barrel as if nothing unusual had happened to him. Except for the bites, scrapes, and redness that showed wherever his skin was uncovered, he seemed perfectly normal.

After a lively visit in the room Gary shared with three other boys, Evan went to determine if they could take him home. He returned with a negative answer.

"Gary has to stay another night. The doctor wants to keep him under observation for a little longer," he told Dawn.

"Is something wrong?"

"No, they just want him to take more fluids and begin eating better before they send him home. It's only a precaution, and he seems to like it here."

They played with Gary and stayed while he picked at his lunch, then the nurse in charge suggested that they leave. The little boy needed rest more than play, and they had to agree that he looked exhausted.

"You'll be going home pretty soon," Evan assured him, but in truth the adults were more troubled about leaving him than he was about being left.

"He's really a trooper," Evan said on their way to the parking lot, and Dawn was sure now that what she heard was fatherly pride.

Still, she delayed asking all the questions that were

stewing in her mind. They had a pleasant lunch, eating slowly in the booth of a small café. They couldn't seem to keep their eyes from meeting and their hands and knees from touching. Letting her true feelings for Evan surface made Dawn almost euphoric, and he seemed as unwilling as she to break the mood with serious discussion.

The car seemed like a private cocoon as they drove through the countryside, closed in as it was to take advantage of the air-conditioner. The fields on either side were starting to burn brown from the impact of the blazing sun, and Dawn realized that harvest time must be near. It was also time for some open questions and honest answers.

"Evan, you said yesterday that Sheila wouldn't come for Gary because you'd paid her."

"Yes, I did."

"But why?"

He slowed the car but didn't stop; the country road was nearly deserted in the heat of the afternoon, and driving took little concentration.

"To get proof that Gary is my son."

"You have proof?"

He braked the car, pulling onto a beaten dirt road that was little more than a path inching its way between two fields of dense cornstalks. Even after he killed the ignition, he stared straight ahead for a long moment.

"Tell me, Evan!"

"I'm trying to decide how," he said with the anguish in his voice apparent.

"Straight out! I'm not a child."

"All right. As soon as I got the letter from Sheila, I called Cliff and told him to make a deal with her."

"Evan, what kind of a deal?"

"I agreed to pay Sheila if she'd furnish immediate proof that Gary was my child and sign an agreement never to attempt to see him or claim him. She had his birth certificate, and Cliff called to verify it the same day. He was born in Cleveland, not Chicago, so it was no wonder we couldn't trace his records without her help."

"I don't believe you knew all this and didn't tell me. I even called Cliff, and he wouldn't say a thing. Why did you keep it from me?"

"I didn't want you to leave."

A faint quiver of his lower lip betrayed the intensity of his feelings, but Dawn was too upset to notice.

"You should have told me. I had a right to know. I brought Gary to you."

"Damn it, Dawn, you're so big on rights! Would you have stayed if you'd known?"

"You should have given me a chance to decide that for myself. I can't believe you've known all this time. You knew the day we played golf?"

"Yes," he said solemnly.

"And you knew when you first mentioned marriage."

"I knew," he said, his voice totally devoid of argument, apologizing with every word and gesture he made.

"I don't understand. It would have changed everything."

"Would it? Gary needs a mother and a father, whether he's mine or not. I was afraid to risk losing you, Dawn. That boy needs two parents; he needs a mother, Dawn."

"That's why you asked me to marry you! How convenient! You gain a son, and a mother to take care of him, in one fell swoop."

Tears blinded her eyes, and she thought the pain would destroy her. It all fell into place. Evan had never said he loved her. It was his son he loved, and she was only a convenient candidate for the role of mother.

"Don't say that!" he begged. "Do you think I was faking when I made love to you? I need you as much as Gary does. Dawn, I'd been so lonely, I nearly went sour on life."

"Of course, you made love to me. What could be more

handy? A warm body in your bed and a full-time baby-sitter!"

All her dreams and happiness, nurtured since Evan had awakened her that morning, exploded in a burst of humiliated anger; she yanked off her seat belt and dashed from the car, too blinded by her pain to realize that there was no place to go, no place but the endless ocean of yellowing stalks that had nearly swallowed up a little boy.

There wasn't a fence to impede her, so she plunged between the tall plants, hearing Evan's car door slam behind her. Her feet sank in powdery dirt as she ran blindly down a closely packed row, cutting over to another row and another, speeding away from Evan without thinking about where she was going. The drying stalks whipped at her face and arms, making her feel as if she were being flayed alive by sadistic executioners.

Her breath was coming in ragged gasps, and her lungs ached as they filled with pollen and dust stirred up by her flight. She could hear Evan's voice calling her name, but her sense of direction abandoned her. The more she broke through parallel rows to escape him, the less she knew where she was.

So breathless she doubted her ability to go another step, she sank to the ground, not knowing that Evan had been following her by the movement of the towering stalks. She sat motionless on the ground, and it was as if the earth had swallowed her.

Evan's voice calling her name was muffled and becoming more distant, but in her agitated state it took her a few minutes to realize that he had bypassed her and was headed in the opposite direction.

The sun barely penetrated between the stalks, but the heat was stifling, every bit as bad as it had been for Gary yesterday. She couldn't be foolish enough to get heat stroke herself; just imagining that Evan would call out search teams to look for her was enough to bring her to her feet. The only important thing at this moment was to put as much distance as possible between Evan and her, but she couldn't do it playing hide-and-seek in a cornfield. Sooner or later she had to return to his house, pack her suitcases, and leave. There was no way to do it without first returning to his car and allowing herself to be driven to his farm. She knew the area well enough now to know it was too far to walk, especially in her fragile shoes, with no hat.

She pushed her way through several rows of stalks before the truth hit her—she had no idea where to go. The car could be parked in any direction. Every row looked just like the one beside it, and the way she needed to go wasn't marked by the slightest clue. She hadn't looked at the sun before she ran into the field, so it didn't offer the guidance she needed now. As humiliating as it was, she was lost.

Either Evan wasn't calling her anymore, or he was too far away from her to be heard. The possibility that he'd left passed through her mind, but she doubted it. He wasn't callous enough to abandon her, and he had too much pride to ask for help in searching for a woman who'd run from him.

Swallowing her own anger and pride, she called his name loudly, standing motionless to hear his reply. There wasn't any. Again and again she moved a few yards and tried calling, but there was no response. Where she had felt ridiculous, she now felt more than a little alarmed. Maybe Evan was punishing her for rejecting his proposal; perhaps he would leave her in the field alone for hours, then return when he thought she'd suffered enough. As if he could hurt her any more than he already had, suggesting that she marry him to become Gary's mother! That they were good together in bed was only a small bonus for him. He needed her to solve the problem of who would care for his son, the son he hadn't acknowledged to her until today.

Just thinking about it made her so furious, she didn't know if she wanted to be found by him. Pushing through the sharp-bladed stalks, inhaling their hot scent and dusty pollen, driven to distraction by the itching and smarting they were causing on her bare arms, she didn't even notice that bitter tears were trickling down her cheeks. Damn Evan Crane!

The long, sinewy creature was only inches from her toe when, as startled as she was, it slithered between two stalks. Dawn's scream was involuntary, piercing the air as surprise added to her fear of snakes.

Even after the long, mottled-brown body disappeared, she stood stark still, too frightened to move. Plunging blindly as she had through row after row of corn, she could easily step directly on that reptile or one like it, and the prospect paralyzed her.

"Dawn!"

Evan's cry was far distant, but fear sharpened her hearing.

"I'm here," she yelled with all her lung power, still not daring to move from the spot.

"Keep calling," he urged her, sounding louder. "I'll follow your voice."

"Over here!"

"Are you all right?"

"No . . . yes. I saw a snake."

"Did it bite you?" His voice was coming closer.

"No."

"Don't worry. It's probably a bull snake. They're harmless."

He was in the next row now, but it wasn't only the snake that kept her from moving toward him. She didn't want to be rescued by him. The closer he came, the sharper her pain became.

186

"Are you okay?" he asked, crashing through the last row that separated them.

Lowering her eyes, she didn't answer. She couldn't. Her throat closed up, and the only sound possible was the wheeze of her quickened breathing and the irregular thump of her heart.

"How could you scare me like this after yesterday?" he demanded, showering weeks of hurt and frustration on her. "Dawn, I asked you to be my wife, share my life. What did I do that was so wrong?"

"You deceived me," she said, raw hatred giving her voice. "You kept me at your home deliberately because you knew Gary was your son, and he needed a mother."

"Oh, God, if I made you believe that, I deserve to be hung," he said wretchedly, standing so close she could see the heaving of his chest. "Look at me!"

Defying him, she kept her head averted, but he moved even closer, cupping her face in hard hands and forcing her to look at him.

"I want you for myself, not Gary," he said in a deep, strangled voice.

"For your afternoon roll in the hay," she cried.

"You blame me for Gary getting lost," he said bitterly. "Why shouldn't you? I blame myself."

"Gary has nothing to do with this!" she insisted, squirming to free herself from his grip. "Don't touch me again."

"You like to be touched!" he argued furiously.

"Not by you!"

"No?"

His lips smashed against hers, sucking her into a vortex of feeling that made her spine go rubbery and her very core burn for him. When she fought him, she fought herself too.

Suddenly going limp, her passiveness stopped him where her struggling hadn't.

"I love you, Dawn," he cried, his voice choked with emotion.

"Evan?"

She wanted to believe him more than she wanted to live, but why had it taken him so long to say it? Was he using the words she'd longed to hear to trap her into staying?

"Don't marry me. I'll hire a woman to take care of Gary. Just don't leave me, Dawn. I'm the one who needs you. I couldn't tell you the truth about Gary and take a chance on having you leave."

"You never told me that you loved me," she said weakly.

"I tried a hundred times, but my bad marriage got in the way. I don't expect you to understand, but in my whole life I'd only told one person I loved her, and I had it thrown back in my face. I was afraid to take that chance again."

"Because you're a forever person," she said, more to herself than him.

"What makes you say that?"

She only shook her head, unconsciously running her sharp-edged fingernails up and down her arms to ease the burning itch.

"Don't do that to yourself," he said, taking her hands in his and looking at her reddened arms.

"Tell me again," she said, trembling at his touch.

"I love you, Dawn, I love you."

He lifted her against him, implanting a deep and tender kiss on her parted lips.

"Marry me," he insisted, releasing her lips only for her answer.

"I couldn't make myself leave you," she said. "It all came to mean nothing—the job, California, my plans."

"Nothing means anything if you don't share it with someone you love."

"Yes."

"Yes, you agree with me, or yes, you'll marry me?" he pressed, holding her against him with tender force.

"I'll marry you," she said, knowing that there was nothing in the world that she wanted more than to be with Evan.

"You can find a job, if you want to," he said. "People here have problems too, and the county should have something in your line. I won't tie you down with Gary."

"For now, I want us to be a family."

"I love you, and I want you, Dawn," he said, summoning the words from the innermost reaches of his being.

"I love you, Evan," she said, hugging him emphatically, "Now, get me out of this cornfield."

Laughing, he scooped her into his arms and took her home.

LOOK FOR NEXT MONTH'S
CANDLELIGHT ECSTASY ROMANCES™

When You Want A Little More Than Romance—

Try A Candlelight Ecstasy!